A
WICKED WOMEN WRITERS
ANTHOLOGY FROM
HORRORADDICTS.NET

EDITED BY
HOLLIE SNIDER

The Wickeds

Copyright © 2012 HorrorAddicts.net

Printed in the United States of America.
Edited by Hollie Snider
Cover art by Masloski Carmen
Layout by Henry Snider

ISBN: 978-1463612702

HorrorAddicts.net

the wickeds

THERE'S A LITTLE WICKED IN ALL OF US

foreward

BY HOLLIE SNIDER

Well, The Wickeds have finally done it. We've put out an anthology designed to help better the world through literacy. Thirteen women have created tales for your reading enjoyment and have agreed to donate all proceeds to LitWorld.org, a charity dedicated to children's literacy around the world. The Wicked Women Writers want to thank all those who purchased this book for their part in making literacy happen.

The ladies would also like to thank all the fans of HorrorAddicts.net and the Wicked Women Writers. Without you all listening and reading our offerings, we'd still be in a dark corner, typing like mad on keyboards, cackling and talking to ourselves. Not that we aren't anyway, but our readers and listeners give us a legitimate reason for doing so, and keep us from being locked away somewhere.

I'd especially like to thank Emerian Rich, creator and hostess of HorrorAddicts.net, for selecting these stories, and Michele Roger, who created the Wicked Women Writers as a place for women horror writers to gather and network, giving us a voice in a male-dominated genre.

We hope you enjoy our little tales!

Yours in Wickedness,

Hollie Snider, Editor

about the wickeds

BY SAPPHIRE NEAL

*H*orror Addicts, it's finally arrived – a book so downright horrifying and utterly wicked, you'll have nightmares for weeks to come. That's right, these pages contain dreadfully addictive tales from the Wicked Women Writers, a tight-knit group of women who love nothing more than telling stories to make you wet yourself. They'll have you scared, laughing, and even lusting within a matter of minutes. This anthology showcases the Wicked Women Writers at their best . . . being Wicked!

From their small group of seven, the WWW has grown to over 20 members, including such names as: Rhonda Carpenter, Laurel Anne Hill, Arlene Radasky, Emerian Rich, Michele Roger, Heather Roulo, and Hollie Snider. The group was actually kick-started by Michele Roger who "came up with the idea for a writing group just for women who write in the horror genre."

Michele explained to me how the Wicked Women Writers got their start. "I was a new writer and trying to get published. Each week, I received some kind of rejection letter. Meanwhile, I was reading short horror stories and listening to podcasts. I realized that I heard or read work from very few women, but

I suspected that there were a lot of women who were trying to get their work out there, like me. I figured that if women were going to have a voice in horror fiction, the best place to start would be to have a collective voice as well as a place to network and support one another. The Wicked Women Writers group started as a little forum. Then, Emz offered to me a page on her HorrorAddicts.net site. I was surprised to see how quickly the group grew over a short time. We've had some real success too, both as individuals and as a group."

Emz, author Emerian Rich, hosts a WWW Challenge on her website every season. The women share their stories, and fans have the chance to vote on their favorite spooky tale. 2010 WWW winner Rhonda Carpenter was excited to share her expectations of future competitions. "We expect each year for there to be more and more contestants. This year we have seventeen in the running which means that next year, if we keep growing like we are, there could be well over twenty free stories for the HA fans to vote on. And that means that the prizes which are awarded to the Lucky Voters will just get bigger too. There's no other way for it to happen. Emz may want to buy stock in a big box company! The prizes are donated by the participating authors and can range from a nice Thank You letter to autographed copies of their books and other cool schwag. I mean, who is the loser here? Nobody!"

According to Emz, the fans fall more and more in love with the Wickeds as time goes by. "Every year we get hundreds of emails about who they think wrote the best Wicked Women Writers story!"

In this anthology, you'll find Rhonda's award-winning story, "Barring Lilith," along with another winning Wicked Women Writer submission, Heather Roulo's, "Graveyard Shift and Reshift." Some of the other stories that can be found here include:

Jennifer Rahn's story, "Fallen," originally podcast on Horror Addicts Episode 50, in the science-fiction horror category. It's told from the perspective of an alien, Tharn, who finds himself cast into the company of a psychotic human, who decides he needs part of Tharn's body. Tharn comes up with some pretty creative notions of how he might exact revenge."

Hollie Snider's, "More Than Kin" was part of the Horror Addicts show a season or two back. She says, "It's my own twist on Washington Irving's classic tale about a not-so-headless horseman."

Michele Roger's, "Santa CLAWS," is "a story about how Mrs. Claus, a young gold-digger, and Elderby, the head elf, discover Santa has been bitten by a werewolf boy whilst delivering toys on Christmas Eve. Chaos comes to life while Santa CLAWS goes on a killing/feasting spree. It's up to Dr. Greg, part vet, part modern van Helsing, and Elderby's army of 'Santa's Helpers' creepy elf robots to bring Santa the Werewolf down before all of the North Pole becomes a homicide scene."

And of course, a story from Horror Addicts' very own hostess, Emerian Rich. "Her story is about an unlikely vampire who is partial to aerobics and pastel sofa cushions rather than coffins and graveyards. When she's stalked by a group of goth kids, she has

to figure out how to stop them from trying to get her gift. This story is sarcastic and will be the comedy relief in a book full of awesome thrillers and spooky tales."

The Wickeds have high hopes for this anthology, as they should. "[They are] extremely excited to bring the WWW work out to the public in text format. The WWW Horror Addicts anthology is not only great for the authors in the way of helping to spread the word about their work, but for the charity receiving the donation of the profits. If the Wicked Women Writers can contribute to literacy, [they] see this as a win-win anthology. None of the ladies are taking any money for their work. It is all going to charity."

The Wicked Women Writers are growing all the time. "The gals are supporting and cheering each other on to what is sure to be imminent success. Story ideas fly through the threads and if you just want to vent about your process or get a great hint on how to podcast, or even talk marketing there is usually a fast reply on the threads. All the new gals are wonderful authors and no one can wait to see what turns out this year for the WWW Challenge."

To quote Emz, "Our community is more about being a woman in a writing genre that is dominated by men. We support each other, share tips, and even help each other. It's kind of like a secret society. We don't have a strange handshake, but if another WWW asks for help, we all chip in." Or, as Michele put it, "It just seemed to me that the sci-fi and horror genres are a bit of a 'boy's club.' There are real marketing reasons why many female writers publish under their initials or a pen name in this area of literature."

The Wicked Women Writers have become more of a force than anyone could have imagined when it started. All that's certain is that the Wickeds will "leave the listener with a satisfying chill in the bones."

SAPPHIRE NEAL is a graphic designer and her writing has been published in literary magazines. Sapphire is the author interviewer for HorrorAddicts.net and plans to successfully infiltrate the advertising world to fund her dream of becoming a published novelist.

forever

BY ARLENE RADASKY

HorrorAddicts.net Episode #08

The door was open.
A breeze carried the odor to wake my memories.
He wore it the last weeks of his life.
His clothing and hair reeked.

My skin crawled as I inhaled.
Recollections wormed their way through my mind.
The lock he had on my soul was complete
Even though he rotted in his grave.

When alive, he never let me outside
Unless he was right there.
If I looked up and saw something that made me smile,
He would pinch, or grab my wrist and squeeze.

At first, my love was adoration
I was moonstruck and unrealizing.
When he turned to pain and anger.
I was trapped, a mouse in a cage.

Every night for one year,
He came home at two or three AM,
Saying it was business
That kept him so long.

I believed.

Six months ago, his wasting started,
I noticed his clothes begun to drape.
By now he was raping me,
and I traveled to other places.

The pain he caused,
Biting my breasts and other ways,
Grew even more intense.

Soon after, he carried the scent home.

It was light at first, incense-like.
Then grew suffocating.
Even his shadow exuded the stench.
I stayed, trapped, a fly on sticky paper.

He never lacked for things.
He owned a successful business.
Money would be no worry when he died,
One more reason to stay through his illness.

He told me
The doctors said the horse of death was not far
He would ride the stallion named Cancer to the finish.
And I should bet on the race.

At the end, he could not go out,
Too weak and pain-ridden.
His cell never left his side
Except to lay by his ear in the end.

I heard the murmurs of chants and conjurations,
Drumbeats seemed close at hand.
He had me plug it into the charger
Its battery-life linked to his.

2

ARLENE RADASKY

He died.
I drank Champagne.
His lawyers visited and laughed
And they told me he'd sold everything.
My name was not on the deeds.

Now, I walk the streets alone.
Just as afraid as before.
I carry my possessions
In a bag from the thrift store.

The sidewalks are my bed,
Which I would readily accept
If I could be rid of him,
Free from the pain and fear.

But he is still here.
He comes in the night.
Some say it is only dreams
But I feel him after I awake.

He sits on the edge of a green field,
A sneer on his face.
He beckons me to come to him
And my feet start his way.

It is at this point I wake up, every time.

Walking today, an alley called my name.
One I have never seen.
I turn left and stumble down,
To find a door open to me.

A door.
An opening.
A beginning.
A new start.

So I believe.

I stop and peer through dim haze,
To see her sitting on the floor.
Her legs crossed, Indian style,
Flickering candles heightening the shadows.

Black Rastafarian dreadlocks,
Hang down her back in disarray.
Her eyes closed and body swaying
To the time of the chant she speaks.

I hear her pray, "Papa Gede"
In her lazy, sing-song rhythm.
Later I learned the God of Death
Was called to take me to the man who died.

I turn to leave,
My heart vibrating a warning.
Her voice hums out a greeting
And my steps stop, mid-stride.

"Hello. I have been waiting for you."

My breath abates.
Time suspends.
Who is she
Who waits for me?

4

ARLENE RADASKY

"Come in, My Love.
I have a message.
The dead leave it,
And ask me to summon you.

I hear your name in my visions,
I read your name in my teacup.
I find your name in the rose petals,
I call your name in my songs.

You must come in
And search for your release
From the dreams that haunt you
The visions of him."

She looks at me with raven eyes.

"How," I ask, "do you know of . . . Him?"
My voice sounds like dead leaves
Crushed underfoot.
Unbelief rules my thoughts.

"He haunts me too," she sings.
It is then I smell the candle scent and smoke.
It rises and fills the small room,
And drifts out the door.

I gag at the odor, the suffocating scent
The same he brought home so many times.
I begin to back out, but she says
"Stop. He hurt me, too."

I sit, cross-legged,
Inside the circle of flame.
Opposite the one who sang to the God of Death,
And listen to her tale.

5

"He came to me,"
She starts,
"To take Death away.
He begged me to save him.

He learned about my cures and curses
From the clubs he used to attend
Many with money would come to me
To ask time to stop."

She went on to the rhythm of a dripping tap,
"I have that power, you know.
Gede has given me his hands to work with.
But only if the trip has not started.

Your husband was too far along.
His boat was half across the river when he came.
The man in black was on the doorstep
And commanded his attendance.

Gede would not give him back."

I tremble when I think
Of what could have been.
His death reversed,
Him still alive.

She continues, "Now, I see your dreams in mine.
How he waits for you to come.
I have an idol, a charm, a few words,
To work what is needed."

6

"Yes!" I answer,
My heart in my throat,
"Please release me
From his omniscient power.

I have nothing to give, he took all I owned."
Then I remember the golden cross
My mother had given me,
Break the chain and hand it to her.

"This is perfect!" she says.
"Now hold this in trade."
And places into my palm
A small, silver ball.

Inside were chimes,
Sounds of angels' voices
When I moved my hand,
Fingers curled around my charm.

"As you sleep,
My sweet one,
Hold it tight.
Do not let it go.

With it
You will be able to speak to him.
Tell him what you want.
That he is not to come to you, anymore."

Her dark eyes never left mine
In all this time.
My heart told me she was true,
My mind was over-ruled.

"How do I thank you?"
I wondered out loud.
"How can I seem grateful enough?
If this works, I will owe you so much."

A smile crept onto her serious face.
"No, Dearie, I will have been paid.
To see a smile on the face of one in the dreams
My riches will be fulfilled."

I started to cry in relief.

"Don't do that, we can't have that,"
She said and touched my shoulder.
"I'll get us a cup of my favorite tea,
We can do with a bit of refreshing."

She stands and disappears
Behind the beaded curtain.
I hear the water fill the teapot
And roll the charm in my hand.

I relax as it sings to me
Its small bells pealing,
Then a question raises its head
Why would she help me so?

The beads part
And she sits the tray down.
Fragrant steam rises from the cups.
All doubts are gone.

I drink deep and long
Of a cloying sweet flavor,
One that urged me to finish
At her insistence.

8

"My tea will give you dreams,
My Dearie,
Visions to seal a bargain."
Her smile seemed less friendly.

I cannot stay upright,
I lay myself down.
She puts a pillow under my head,
And whispers in my ear.

"Hold on to the charm, My Dear,
Do not open your hand.
Look back and see yourself,
You are attached here."

"What?" I asked. "Attached?"
The meadow is in front of me,
He sits on the other side.
My breathing is faster than ever before.

I turn and see myself,
On the floor, chest rising with breath.
She is seated next to me
Still whispering into my ear.

I feel him get up
I feel him stand and stretch.
As if he's been waiting
A very long time.

I watch him start across the grass.
I yell, "Leave me alone!"
I cringe when he doesn't stop
And then he laughs.

Twisting back to see myself,
Not understanding why,
My hand has fallen open,
The charm rolled out to the floor.

My chest has stopped moving.
It was then I hear her say,
Words that seal my future,
Words that burn my skin.

"He came to me but when we found
We could not stop his death.
He asked that I make sure he kept
The one thing that gave him pleasure.

"'Tis you, My Dearie.
You are his one desire.
He paid for me to summon you
And send you to his side.

"The charm you hold
And the tea you drank,
Were the end of our bargain.
You are his forever. See him smile?

And now I take my fortune and go back to Haiti.
My mother is ill and I must tend her.
Good-bye to both of you.
And enjoy your time together!"

I feel his hand on my wrist and scream.

ARLENE RADASKY

ARLENE RADASKY loves history. There are so many mysteries in history out there, and she would like to provide answers to some. Her first novel, The Fox, is about an ancient couple and modern archeologists. It is available free to download in several places to all readers. She loves to write poetry and short stories and has fun recording them. She has two grown daughters who, between them, have given her three grandsons. She lives in Southern California with her husband and cats. She often goes to the beach for inspiration. Find out more about Arlene at www.Radasky.com.

the hunger

BY LINDA CILETTI
HorrorAddicts.net Episode #42

*P*ain knifed his gut. He had to feed.

Damon swept a hungry look over bleak city streets, his wolfish eyes dark with need. Large, calloused paws padded soundlessly through the winding alleyways – his hunting ground.

People disappeared all the time. Transients and homeless misfortunates who would not be missed vanished without a trace – not an ounce of flesh, a drop of blood, or a splinter of bone. His kind made sure of that.

Brilliant stars faded as black night lightened to indigo blue. Crisp, pre-morning dampness settled dew on the cold, concrete jungle and the flora oases scattered throughout, blanketing the coarse hairs on his back.

The hunger grew.

Damon paused, lifted his muzzle, and sniffed the air. Nothing. He hastened his gait, ran as though his life depended on it.

It did. He had to feed.

Bitter cold had driven homeless transients to places of warm refuge. The streets lay empty of prey. Again he sniffed, catching the aroma of fresh baked bread as it filtered out from vented ovens. Bakers

13

awakened first, preparing their goods for the early morning rush of a ravenous public.

He was ravenous.

If he did not soon feed, the night would pass and his stomach would twist and grind until he'd be forced to beg for mercy from a god who had abandoned him – who had allowed him to fall into this half life of man and beast. He no longer believed in God. Yet when the hunger came upon him, when the pain consumed him, he could not help but cry out for relief. Perhaps he believed in God after all. But God was not his friend, and any relief was fleeting, a temporary reprieve until the hunger returned.

How soon, he could not say. Time lapse between feedings varied. Sometimes a month. Sometimes a week. Sometimes merely a day. Quality of flesh and blood determined fullness. The younger the better. But not too young. Nourishment needed to mature like fine wine, definitely past adolescence, but prior to the breaking down of the body.

Nourishment. Damon lifted his nose and breathed in a familiar bouquet. Human. His heart hammered against his chest. Picking up speed, he followed the scent. Each pounding step echoed in his ears, a ticking clock counting down the seconds to satiation.

Some might call him a vampire, some a werewolf. He snorted at the misguided beliefs. He was both. And neither.

Humans and their silly misconceptions. Hunger and night prompted his change. No full moon needed, though the revealing light of a full moon made it easier to hunt. And though a silver bullet would assuredly stop his heart, a lead one would as well.

Damon slowed his pace and sniffed again. Human scent thickened in the air like a dense fog. His prey was close.

Anticipation heightened his senses. He could almost taste the hot, coppery sweetness of blood on his tongue, smell its metallic scent in the near-still breeze. Blood pulsed in his veins and sounded in his ears like the hollow beat of a warm and meaty heart. Saliva slid through razor-sharp fangs and roiled slowly over firm canine lips. Pangs of need speared his gut and he loosed an anguished howl.

Suddenly, the air grew thick with fear and he followed the scent, keeping to the shadows cast by tall, ornate street lamps with hunched backs and hanging heads. A purring carriage rolled easily by, modern and lacking horses. Brilliant light shot from its eyes, piercing the darkness, illuminating the road and its parallel walk. Damon sank deep into a shadowed alcove until the carriage passed.

His throat ached, parched and dry and craving blood. He was a beast, a lycanthropic blood-lusting vampire that could not be satiated. At least, not for long. In all his years, several hundred at least, mankind had not assigned a name to those like him.

Damon curled his lips despite the agony. His kind left no trace. They ingested and drank, consuming the kill until not a crimson drop of blood or sliver of flesh remained. Their thoroughness granted them invisibility. No body. No slaughter. No existence.

Damon sniffed the air. Anxiety no longer carried on the breeze. The scent of blood melded with warming, pre-dawn smells venting from towering dwellings of concrete and brick; acrid smells of burning oil and coal, week-old garbage waiting pickup, and urine of both man and feral beasts cast out from domesticity.

Damon stilled. A mistake. Pain knifed his gut and he howled loudly. Again fear rent the air. Strong. Acute. His senses heightened. Thick, hot saliva filled his mouth and oozed in stealthy silence from the corners of his lips. Damon turned his elongated head, cocked the furred length of pointed ears until the fine hairs dusting their insides bristled, and listened.

Footsteps rang in the crisp pre-morning air. Staccato beats. Hurried beats. Damon's long dark tongue slid over his teeth to lick the spittle from his lips. They tasted of blood – his blood as his stomach ulcerated at its lack of repast. Time ran short. Soon dawn would light the sky and his body would shift to another form. The human form. And he would not live out the day. He had to feed.

Damon sniffed the air and pattered softly. Suddenly a familiar smell struck him and he fought to recall its source. He could not. Hunger consumed him, repressing memories in a shroud of black until only one thought remained – to feed.

A splash of gold touched on the horizon. His gut wrenched, throat burned. Still he managed one last parched howl – one final attempt to raise the level of fear so high that, were he sightless, he could find his prey.

His howl achieved its goal. Quickened footsteps broke into a run. His heart leapt. Vibrant energy ripped through him, easing his pain with the thrilling anticipation of the kill. Had he been able, he would have cried out in pure elation. Instead, he circled around a nearby alley and waited.

She sprinted through the alley, clad in white, long legs moving with ease and grace, and a desperation to cross the threshold of the bakery's back door. She was meaty, not plump. Good. He hated the oily feel of oozing fat on his tongue. Lean protein, that's where the power was. The strength. The pain-quenching satisfaction.

Damon crouched low and readied to pounce.

She slipped her key in the door.

Damon sprang, knocking her back and pinning her under his weight.

Large and grotesquely formed, his solid wolfish girth pinned her to the ground. In shocked silence, she stared up at him.

Despite his pain, he studied her.

The forceful strike knocked the breath from her lungs, forcing it up a throat that could not release.

Her eyes, hollow and wide and filled with fright, stared up at him, twin clouded moons shadowed in dusk.

His lips curled. Her fear intoxicated him and fed his deepest need.

Sparkling gemstones glimmered on her ears. She was no transient or homeless wanderer, but she would have to do. Hunger scorched his gut and filled his throat with a numbing heat that rose to

encompass every sense – sight, sound, taste – until he felt nothing but the intensity of his need. He could not wait another day.

Damon stared down at the smooth curve of her neck, then shifted his sharp gaze to a laceration off her bared shoulder where a fang had snagged her flesh. A thin trail of blood seeped from the shallow wound and dribbled down her arm, its coppery scent coiling over and around him, binding him in a desperate lover's hold.

His tongue lolled out and lapped its heat.

Intense energy tore through him and he closed his eyes, raised his head, and released a rapturous howl. Every muscle tensed, flesh rippled in lascivious bliss. Blood raced through his veins. In all his kills, never had he felt such pure sexual energy.

A lewd growl tore from his throat as he lowered his head and bared his teeth.

Then he recognized her. The woman who had stolen his human heart.

But he wasn't human now. He was a mutant wolfish beast who needed blood to quench his thirst and flesh to satisfy his hunger – a fiend, ravenous and hurting and desperate to survive.

A strangled squeak passed the clench of her throat. Damon stared at that throat, soft and pale, its carotid artery pulsing beneath sweet tender flesh. Drool slid from his lips and landed on her cheek. Pain ripped through him and he opened his mouth, then paused, a caged conscience breaking through his baser need. She was all the goodness of mankind in one lithe and beautiful body. Generous, kind, gentle, loving.

Loving.

His fevered brain struggled to remember.

He loved her.

Tenseness left his body. He knew what he had to do. Freeing her from his weight, Damon gave her leave. Then his eyes shifted to the slit on her arm – a slit that damned her to a half life of blood lust and regret. A life of hell. A life like his.

No!

Damon looked down at her, his golden eyes dark with regret, his throat knotted. A salty tear slid down his muzzle, then he succumbed to the darkness, bared his teeth, and ripped out her throat.

LINDA CILETTI is the author of Draegon's Lair, an epic award winning historical novel; KnightStalker, a contemporary time travel; and Dream of the Archer, a historical paranormal time travel. Her short stories include all of the above and horror. For more on Linda, visit her website at www.LindaCiletti.net

Barring Lilith

BY RHONDA R. CARPENTER
MOST WICKED 2010
HorrorAddicts.net Episode #49

*T*he laptop blinked to life. Jack's parents were finally gone and hadn't, for once, dragged him to their yearly revival retreat. His excuse had been so well-planned. The son of a pastor and a God-crazed mother, Jack Jerkins, at sixteen, learned early on to keep his lies very close to the truth. "Give the 'rents what they expect and you can get away with murder." They were gone less than five minutes before the stereo speakers strained under the hammer of death metal. The guys had been called, beer and supplies were on the way. He carried the laptop to the hallway then down the stairs.

He closed the cellar door behind him. At the bottom of the rickety wooden stairs, Jack set the computer on the washing machine. Jack moved the boxes off the old tattered throw rug in the corner, exposing a crudely drawn circle on the floor in black paint. Dust lifted in the filtered rays of light as he rolled the carpet back. The sound of his operating system engaging made his heart pound in his chest. He executed several key strokes and entered four passwords in quick succession. The file opened and he studied the scanned image from a hundred-year-old grimoire.

21

The King of the Demons, Asmodeus filled the screen. The image portrayed his wavy, dark hair blowing in the wind and a lecherous glint in his ebony eyes. Long and muscular, he lounged upon a throne of fire, wings unfurled. Wild animals stood by his side in fierce poses. The head of a lion was to his right, a great horned ram on his left. The head of a black bull hovered behind and above him, but the most ardent of all was a colossal scaled snake wrapped around the demon king's legs until it became a part of him. The serpent's head stood erect at the demon's groin like a penis, jaws unhinged and fangs exposed.

Jack shuddered in apprehension, ripping his gaze away from the image. He scrolled to the next page. Ornate writing filled the screen surrounding a circular symbol in the center of the page. His eyes moved between the screen and the circle on the floor. They needed four to complete the spell. Where the hell were the guys, he thought.

The next page still took his breath away, even though he'd seen it a thousand times. The image of Lilith seared his retinas. Jack's flesh undulated over tense muscles. Goose bumps rose slowly; not the kind created from cold but those that came when he was aroused.

He ran his finger down the screen, following the curve of her round hip. Hope darted in his mind, chased away by foreboding thoughts of Asmodeus' wrath if they were not triumphant tonight. Jack sighed, looking at Lilith's likeness, and touched himself sending a tingle from his groin to his thighs. His cock throbbed beneath his touch as muscles he could not control clenched and puckered.

Philip Morehead swung his Geo into Max Poker's shabby apartment complex. He honked twice waited a few seconds and flashed the headlights. Matt Urbate and Max trotted out to the car, backpacks in tow.

"'Bout time, Morehead," Max said, slapping his palm on the hood of the car.

"Yeah, where the hell have you been?" Matt chimed in while he slid into the back seat and punched the driver in the arm.

"Fuck you, Masturbate, I had to wait for some asshole to buy the beer. Dad's stock was running low."

Max extracted a bottle of Jim Beam from his backpack and waved it in the air. "Good ol' Mom never lets me down. But the bitch made me clean the kitchen for half a fifth."

The Geo sped out of the parking lot and down the street. "Get a peep of that moon." Philip pointed as they wound their way along the sparsely lit road that led out of town. The moon sat low in the sky, a waning sliver of silver. "You got what we need, Matt?"

"You know I do, and a special little something for the celebration."

"Oh, yeah?" Max asked.

"Went to visit Uncle Pothead." He snickered. "He pulled out a stash box. Ya know, he thought he'd show me somethin' about being a man. When he passed out I took this." He handed the baggy forward.

"Damn. That must be a quarter." The bag was opened and Max stuck his nose inside. "Dude, that's some dank weed."

"Swee-ta," Philip said. "But did you get everything that we need to call the corners and make this bitch ours?"

"Chill, Morehead, I got it all. We're set."

The car pulled off the road, swung right and came to a stop under an old oak tree. As they got out of the car, Max huffed. "Shit you can hear the music from here. Jack-off is going to get us busted for sure."

Jack almost jumped out of his skin when the stereo went dead. He zipped his pants and struck the keyboard closing the file. Then he slapped the laptop lid closed and reached for the rug. But, the sound of multiple sets of footsteps and the guy's voices stopped him in mid movement. He realized he was holding his breath and let the air in his lungs out with measured deliberation while he headed for the steps. "Down here," he called. "Remember to lock the door."

The moon waned and she could feel the itch grow stronger. She rose with a stretch of her pale, sleek body and slid gracefully from black silk sheets to the plush fur rug at her bedside. Lilith tipped a goblet of blood red wine to her lips, drinking deeply. A delicate hand

24

grasped an amber bell. The hollowed stone gleamed in the candlelight as the clapper stuck several times with a resounding ring.

The briefest of moments passed before the double doors swung open, giving her just enough time to seat herself at the gilded dressing table.

A flurry of incubus servants entered. Each carried a silver tray with an ornately carved domed cover concealing its contents. Plump incubus bodies dashed frantically from one side of the room to the other. They were bare except for a flap front and back of sheer black fabric that veiled their obvious maleness. They entered with eyes downcast because to look into the crystalline grey eyes of their mistress's would certainly mean a horrid fate that did not include any tactile pleasure.

Lilith held out her arms and two small demons, her favored Ignig and Omag, washed her from fingertips to breasts.

Each shivered with excitement. Their erections grew with every stroke of their stubby hands on her pale luscious skin. Pointy-toothed grins spread across pitted faces while yellow on yellow gazes roamed her body, careful not to meet her eyes.

Ignig's excitement grew stronger as he drizzled water over her round breast and he giggled with joy as her nipples rose to his tongue's scaly touch. He licked the water from her bosom.

She responded to his touch, arching her back so he could take the whole left breast into his mouth. His mind roared with excitement.

I please my mistress, I do. I do. See her rise to me!

Unable to help himself, Ignig pulled at his twisted cock with his free hand.

Omag was no less excited, but he wanted more than Lilith's breast. He wanted her to touch him. Even if it was by accident, he would take the attention she paid him as a reward. The loincloth at his waist stretched and protruded, grazing her outer thigh. He wiggled back and forth, and sucked at her right breast like a hungry baby. In his excitement, he lost all control sinking tiny sharpened fangs into the pink skin around her hardened nipple.

She grabbed his pointy ear and pulled.

"Release," she ordered through gritted teeth, none too kindly.

He whimpered and shook his head as he ejaculated onto the ground.

"No, you fool. Release your bite. You've broken the skin." She glared into the mirror, seeing the five pin pricks of blood trickle from his teeth. When his mouth was clear of her breast, she smacked him hard across the face. "You will clean up that mess." She pointed to the floor at his feet.

"Yes, Mother." Omag grabbed a cloth but before he bent to the ground Lilith snatched it from his hand. "With your tongue – every drop."

Omag nodded under the pressure of her palm, grinding his pimply face into his own emissions. When he had finished, he looked up, not meaning to meet her gaze. The grey of her eyes was the last thing he saw before his body burst into flames and exploded into a green haze of vapors. Lilith's deep, throaty laugh filled the room.

"I made you. I made you all. And I can do with you as I please if you do not please me. Ephin you are now my right."

Ephin, slightly taller than the others, almost burst. He reminded himself with each stroke of her skin, Don't look in her eyes, don't look in her eyes. She made you and she can make you go poof. No more Ephin, nope,nope, no more. Poof!

"Folic, the brush."

"Yes, Mistress. You are glorious, Mistress." Folic hissed the words. He removed a golden horsehair brush from his tray and stroked her raven-colored hair from scalp to tip.

Several of the other incubi gathered trays of food and drink. Others laid several choices of negligees out on the freshly made bed, awaiting Lilith's choice. Still others attended to Lilith's other insatiable needs.

Folic replaced the large brush, retrieving a much smaller one from his tray. He groomed the bush of pubic hair at her groin. He whispered as he stood back to admire his work. "Ppppperfect, is my mistress. Yes, she is."

Ignig and Ephin reached the tips of her toes at the same moment as if they had shared these responsibilities for decades. But, the truth was they were only created two breeding cycles before and soon would be replaced with a fresher smelling brother.

Lilith strutted to the garments ready for her inspection. She passed by the virginal white. Not my style, she thought. The midnight black lace was fingered momentarily. Didn't I wear this last time?

She stood before the sheer emerald green full-length gown. "This," she stated flatly.

Hemmin held the choice aloft for Lilith. He swallowed drool before it slipped from his cracked lips while he tried not to ingest the straight pins gripped there. She stepped into the silkiness. Hemmin rushed to the step stool, sucking at his spittle, and murmured, "Such an excellent selection, Mistress." He pulled the laces taut at the curve of her back then adjusted the off the shoulder sleeves. "Sssso . . . pretty, Mistress."

"Who has my list of humans?" She turned. Hemmin teetered on the stool. Stubby arms flailed like a windmill in a storm. She looked down to see what the commotion was. Pleading creased his face as his eyes met the grey of Lilith's eyes. Flames encompassed Hemmin's boil-covered body, then he was green vapor.

With a wave of her slender hand, the vapor vanished. "The list."

Scribb jumped forward. "Mistress." He bowed at the waist in his formal way, removing the ornate domed lid. She snatched the parchment roll. Scribb backed up with each bow. The scroll rolled open and Lilith read the names of the young men she would target this waning moon cycle.

"Jack Jerkins, Philip Morehead, Max Poker and Matt Urbate," she read aloud. "Ah, yes. In the prime of puberty. . . . They will be excellent donors for my future children and, if turning them thwarts the man upstairs – all the better. My great lord will enjoy the irony."

The itch grew stronger now that none of her

28

incubi touched her. Not a normal itch, but that of a female cat in heat or chigger bite; the kind where a tiny bump triples in size and oozes bloody fluid when scratched, only to discover scratching makes the itching that much worse.

The Jim Beam bottle passed from boy to boy around the circle as they worked. Jack carefully read the spell. Max positioned black and red candles in the spaces between north, south, east and west. Philip and Matt finished painting the complicated symbol. Then each of them took aloeswood shavings, cinnamon, and myrrh, measuring each into the brass bowls at their feet.

"Next is the dragon's blood. Four pinches, no more. Do you all have your parchment?" Jack's hand held a vial of dragon's blood at the ready.

"Let me get this straight, we write what we want from Lilith, right?" Matt's brain was fuzzy from the JB and his tongue felt thick when he spoke.

"Masturbate, you're a freaking dope. Poker, you explain it," Philip jibbed.

"Knock it off. The first part calls the wife of Asmodeus, Lilith, to us. The second part of the spell is to hold her here to do our bidding. That's where the parchment comes in. You have to write, in dragon's blood, what you want from Lilith, fold it four times, then draw the barring symbol on the back. Each parchment goes in a different corner. That should

bind her here," Jack said seriously.

"What if the Lord of Lust is not so keen on us snatching his bitch?" Max asked.

"The adder's tongue will protect us from him," Jack declared.

Matt's eyes grew wide. "Yeah? I ain't sure I want to fuck with a demon hell bent on revenge."

Jack carefully set the dragon's blood in front of him. He turned the laptop screen so they all had a good view of their desires. The boys stared at Lilith's likeness. Each of their minds ran wild with seductive fantasies.

In one, she moaned passionately. In another, full breasts swung just out of lips' reach. In yet another, Lilith's warm lips parted and took an engorged penis between them. In the last mind, she dominated the teen, teasing him until he erupted with pleasure. Jack snapped the laptop closed.

"Anyone want out?" Jack asked.

"No, man, I am in," Phillip said.

"Yeah, me too," Max announced.

"If you're sure the adder's tongue will work," Matt said, "then, by all means, bring the bitch on." He tipped the Jim Beam bottle up and passed it on.

Jack wasted no time. He wrote, folded, drew, and handed the vial to Matt. When the dragon's blood was back in Jack's hand, he carefully set it aside and retrieved the adder's tongue infusion prepared four weeks earlier. The liquid was thick and stringy, the color of ragweed in bloom. He poured it into a pewter chalice. The smell from the cup permeated the room.

Each boy drank deeply, turned and passed the

cup then lit a black candle. Together they chanted, "Lilith, Mother of the Millions, we invite you to our circle, no other shall appear."

Then they lit the red candles one at a time as they opened themselves to the power of the corner that was theirs.

"Powers of the North," Jack said lifting his hands in the air. "Infuse me with your powers. Surround me with wisdom."

A wind rushed through the basement.

Philip lifted his arms and said," Powers of the South, bring your power to me and surround me with your wisdom."

The flame from each candle grew with Jack's wind.

"Powers of the East, infuse me with your powers and surround me with your wisdom." Matt held his hands above his head. The hose on the back of the washing machine burst and water sprayed across the room then abruptly stopped.

Max shook in his Converse shoes, but held his hands up and, with a commanding tone, said, "Powers of the West infuse me with your powers and surround me with your wisdom." The concrete floor cracked beneath his feet and dank rich earth rose from the fissure.

When it was a pile about two feet deep, and the other boys could no longer see Poker's feet, there was a collective exhale.

As one they chanted, "Wind, Fire, Water and Earth, spirits of the North, South, East, and West join as one. We call the corners. We call to the Mother of the Millions. Demoness of Seduction, we invite you

into our circle." Over and over they said the words.

Lilith's smile increased as the moon reached its apex. "I'm coming, boys." She sashayed to the balcony and stepped into nothingness, leaving only the ring of her alluring laughter on the night's cool breeze.

The basement exploded in a flash of light. Smoke filled the room until the boys could not see each other. Time ceased for them.

Hairs on Jack's arms stood at attention. A ripple of fear swept the length of his body. Panic rose like bile in Max's throat. Philip laughed hysterically while Matt fell to his knees and whimpered.

Lilith stood before them. Her pale skin shimmered even though nothing more than candlelight flickered in the room. Every inch of her was perfect. Her hair glistened blue-black, accentuating stunning grey eyes. The emerald green of her flowing floor-length gown was transparent, exposing the tuft of hair at her groin. Long slender arms swayed to unheard music followed by an exotic gyration of her hips as she spun past each young man.

"I am Lilith and I have come for you, all of you."

To Jack, her voice was sweet and endearing. To Matt, her voice was soothing and almost maternal.

For Philip, there was a touch of nasty playfulness in her tone, and for Max, it was a statement of irrefutable fact that was accented by her palm connecting with his cheek.

Moments ticked by as each boy's fantasy was delivered. When each had climaxed, the smoke in the room cleared.

Lilith stood regally before the group of naked youths.

"Your needs are satiated," she said not waiting for a response. She knew she'd exceeded their wildest needs, meager though they were. "Now, my boys, you shall give me what I desire."

"Anything," panted Max. "Just name it."

"Yes, my love," cooed Jack.

"All that is mine is yours," Philip agreed.

"Command me, Mistress." Matt knelt at her feet licking her toes.

Jealousy filled Jack's mind and he lashed out at Philip. "She's mine and you can't have her." He screamed.

"Bullshit, Jackoff she's mine." Philip threw the first in a series of punches that doubled Jack up and left him cowering on the ground.

"I won't share her." Max lunged forward and pummeled Philip and Jack. A blur of punches were exchanged. Blood flew through the air. They wrestled in a heap on the ground, screaming.

"She's mine."

"No mine."

"Get away from her. She's mine."

All the while, Matt licked Lilith's feet. He nibbled

at her toes and caressed her calves.

Lilith shook her head in disgust.

So easy, she thought. Humans are such weak creatures. Look at them squabble over lusts they have not even experienced.

"I tire of the bickering. I will have their seed, my pet." Her voice echoed in Matt's mind.

She waved her hand in the air. When the puff of smoke cleared, she held the handle of a golden bucket. She reached inside and drew out an ornate dagger. She handed them to Matt. The golden hilt glinted in his hand and rubies pulsated in its ornate handle.

"Bring me their testicles." She hissed the command.

A flash of red lit his eyes as he advanced on his friends. The jagged blade sliced Jack's throat in one clean motion. A spray of blood covered the walls.

Matt turned on Philip who had Max on the ground smashing his head on the concrete floor even though his skull was split wide open and chunks of brain flew with every impact. Blood dripped from the dagger blade, leaving a trail from Jack's corpse to Philip and Max. Matt plunged the knife through his friend's back.

Philip fell forward gasping for air. Bubbles of red-tinged spittle formed, exploded then disappeared on his lips.

Matt twisted the hilt and pulled the knife free, making a strange sucking sound. Philip convulsed, then stopped moving. With a precision Matt didn't know he possessed, he castrated Jack placing his prize in the bucket and moved back to the other two.

With a shove of Matt's foot, Philip rolled off Max's dead body. He took Max's sack in one hand. After two precise cuts, Matt dropped his friend's testicles into the pail with a thud.

Matt turned on Philip taking his scrotum in his hand. He cut Philip's nut sack free, placing it into the bucket at his side. Just for an instant, when Matt's eyes met Philip's, there was a moment of clarity. Matt hesitated just long enough for Philip to whisper with his dying breath. "Adder's Tongue."

Matt's mind raced. The pewter goblet was within reach. With his back to his mistress, he lifted it to his lips and took all of the mixture into his mouth. He stood and turned to present his gifts to his mistress, but, as feared she was not alone.

Asmodeus was next to Lilith, seated in a chair amidst the carnage, one enormous hand held out in a silent command to bring the bucket to him.

Matt proudly strutted toward them, bucket in one hand, knife in the other, and cheeks filled with the adder's tongue mixture.

He bowed at the waist, holding out the bucket to the extended hand.

"So, you thought to have my wife?" Asmodeus' voice thundered.

Matt's head came up suddenly and he spit the concoction into the demon king's face.

Asmodeus laughed. "Did you get that from some spell book?" His laughter was stronger. "You should never believe the spells you read in a book, boy." He turned to Lilith. "I will give you this, my love, he has spirit. You may keep him as a pet. Maybe he will last

longer than the incubi, aye?" His maniacal laughter filled Matt's ears.

Lilith patted Matt on the head like she would have a pet dog, "You are lucky he didn't kill you." She slipped a studded collar around Matt's neck and clipped a chain to her wrist with a snap. "Carry the seed," she commanded, then tugged at the collar.

RHONDA R. CARPENTER is the founder of Lifefirst.com. She is an author, clinical hypnotherapist, handwriting expert, dream analyst, and professional psychic. Her first novel, The Mark of a Druid, is available in audio, e-book, and print. Rhonda is the co-founder of Podioracket. com, where you can learn all about the new Podiobooks. com authors and indie authors from all over the world. She lives on a secluded ranch in Southeastern Oklahoma where she enjoys raising chickens and cows. She is happily married and the mother of four boys, all grown and on their own, and recently a first-time grandmother.

remember me

BY JERI UNSELT

HorrorAddicts.net Episode #48

*E*ven after all these years, I can still see her staring at me, blood running down her cheeks, holding the blade, ready to end her life or mine.

The story of Bloody Mary was an obsession for Sonja. She wanted our band, Sparrow Phoenix, to do a prog-concept album about the legend. It wasn't until we, and the rest of the band, spent the weekend at a place called Kenyon Rock, where everything supposedly occurred, that we saw just how obsessed she was.

I managed to escape her bloody wrath with my life and two of my bandmates. It had taken me twenty long years to finally get myself back on track, I thought it was all behind me, but that one night, she had invaded my dreams and I woke up screaming.

The sudden sound of my cell phone ringing seemed to bring me back to life. I glanced at the caller ID and sighed. "Darla." I picked it up and clicked on send. "This better be good, Darla."

"Melodie," she said.

I glanced at my alarm clock. "It's two in the morning, Darla. You know Saturdays are my days to sleep in."

"I'm sorry," she whispered softly. "I just wanted to call and say goodbye."

"Goodbye." I sat up and turned on my light. "What do you mean, goodbye?"

"Because I'm going to die soon."

My jaw dropped. "Why would you say that?"

"Because as soon as Adam finds me," Darla explained.

"What?" Adam and Darla had been in a relationship for three years and they seemed deeply in love. What she said didn't make a bit of sense. "What happened?"

"I don't know," she begin to explain. "Everything was so great, that was until he called her name."

"Darla?" I called out to her, but I suddenly couldn't hear anything. "Darla, answer me!"

"I'm here."

Relief came over me as her voice returned.

"I should've listened to you Melodie, we never should've come here. I'm so sorry."

The relief I felt earlier left me. "Where are you Darla?" My chest heaved. "Please tell me you're not at Kenyon Rock?"

Darla's voice quivered. "I am."

"Oh, God!" I fell backwards against the bed as I saw Sonja's image glaring at me. "Darla, you've been told never ever go there! You know what happened."

"Adam said it would be all right," she answered. "He said it was all an urban legend."

Just hearing those awful words made me grit my teeth in anger. If what was happening at Kenyon Rock was all an urban legend, why were people dying? I

38

took a deep breath and decided that this wasn't the time to be angry with Darla. "It's gonna be okay," I promised. "Where exactly are you? Are you close to the main road?"

"No."

"Well, then, how far are you?" I asked. "When I was there, everything was within walking distance."

"Pretty far." I heard Darla collapse. "I don't wanna die, Melodie."

"Then don't give up!" I screamed. "Please!"

"You were right," Darla continued to say. "Bloody Mary took control of Adam and killed everyone here."

I nodded remembering just how fragile and vulnerable Sonja was to Mary's evil control. If only I knew then what I knew now. "I know, Darla, let's just concentrate on getting you out of there."

"No."

"Everything will be okay," I assured her.

"You can't," Darla cried out.

"Yes I can, Darla," I replied. "I'll help you."

"No Melodie!"

"Why not?"

"Because," Darla said lowering her voice. "He's here."

I gasped as I heard the thunderous pounding of a door. " Darla!"

"He's gonna kill me," she cried out.

"Find a place to hide," I ordered her. "Hang up the phone and find a place to hide, damn it!" I couldn't hear anything in fact, it was so silent that the volume of crickets chirping was up full blast.

All of a sudden, the silence was broken by a blood

curdling scream. "Darla?"

"Oh no."

"What is it?" I heard the cutting of wood.

"Adam's trying to break down the door with an axe," Darla quietly explained. "He knows I'm here. I'm sorry, Melodie."

"I'm the one that should be sorry, Darla," I answered. "Not you."

"He's almost here, oh, God!"

If only I hadn't done the research on Bloody Mary, I thought. "Darla!" If only I could've talked Sonja out of the obsession. "Darla, answer me!" There was no response.

Silence returned with a vengeance.

Then the door opened.

"Darla!"

"Adam!" I heard her scream. "Please! Please, no!"

The phone fell to the floor. I was immediately sickened and repulsed by the thrashing of what could have been blood and the tearing of flesh that belonged to my dear, sweet friend Darla.

"No." I fell to the floor, sobbing like there was no tomorrow. Once again, couldn't hear anything on the other end. That was until I heard heavy breathing.

"Adam, you better find the deepest hole you can find, because if I find you, I'm gonna kill you. You hear me!"

"Hello, Melodie." A voice spoke on the other line that sounded nothing like Adam.

I shuddered as I realized it was someone whose voice I hoped to never hear again.

"Sonja?"

40

JERI UNSELT

"No, not Sonja. Remember me?"

JERI UNSELT is a native of Colorado who has been writing stories ever since childhood. She started podcasting her first novel, Inner Demons, in 2008. The print book will be released in 2012 alongside a podcast prequel, Inner Demons: Turmoil. She is a member of the Wicked Women Writers and has been featured on several HorrorAddicts. net episodes. To find out more about Jeri, go to: www. JeriUnselt.com

pretty proud

BY R.E. CHAMBLISS
HorrorAddicts.net Episode #49

When Justin Johnstone's chimpanzee ripped the face off of Chelsey Sullivan, a teenage girl, my boss, Eleanor Winslow decided it was time for a second assistant.

Justin Johnstone, otherwise known as the Pop Prince, was Eleanor's biggest client. He'd had a slew of hit songs in the early 90s but had been alienating his fans since Y2K, becoming first eccentric and then outright bizarre. Which is why he'd hired Eleanor — she had a knack for making dull CEOs look interesting and charismatic, flighty actresses appear more stable, and geeky dot com-ers seem more personable to the main stream public.

Eleanor specialized in reinventing the notorious, however. When the rich and powerful found themselves arrested for cocaine possession, or were heard making racial slurs, or got caught in an affair, they called Finesse Image Consulting, Eleanor's boutique firm, to try to reverse the damage.

I'd been Eleanor's assistant for three years and had helped her repair the reputations of countless celebrities. I loved the image consulting business and wanted to learn everything I could from Eleanor. We were so alike — smart, ambitious, no-nonsense —

not tied up in our appearance like so many of our gender. True she was pushing 50 and I was 25 years younger, but otherwise I felt like we were the same soul in two different bodies.

Within a week of starting at Finesse, I traded in my Dell laptop and bought a Mac because Eleanor had one. I moved to a condo near her Beverly Hills home. I switched to her bank. When I found out Eleanor had a third-degree black belt in Tae-Kwon-Do, I signed up for lessons the same afternoon. Martial arts turned out to be the one interest of hers that didn't appeal to me, though. Way too time consuming. Still, I knew she believed women derived confidence from being physically powerful and able to protect themselves, so I bought a Glock and carried it loaded in my purse. Now we both could produce lethal force at will.

Eleanor was always very choosy about her clients and turned people down regularly. "Some messes are too big even for me!" she would say. But the clients she accepted, while not always thrilled with her approach or blunt demeanor, quit complaining once they saw the results.

After Justin Johnstone's chimpanzee, BoBo, went on the rampage against poor Chelsey Sullivan, however, Eleanor was stuck. Justin was already a client – and Eleanor didn't like to turn her back on a client.

"There's got to be a way to spin this," she said the day the story broke. She tapped at her front teeth with a pen, thinking.

"Beth, we're going to need to bring someone new into Finesse. I have a feeling you're going to be key

44

when it comes to this mess, but there is no way you'll be able to do it alone. I need you on full time social media. Tweeting, Facebook, the Prince's website and blog. We'll start changing the public's perceptions online, and then we'll have an easier time with TMZ, People and Entertainment Weekly. You won't be able to handle the phones and the schedule as well. I'll find someone to help you."

"I can put up an ad on Monster if you'd like."

"No, that's all right. I'll contact some friends and see if they know anyone suitable."

I had mixed feelings about Eleanor wanting a second assistant. I liked that it was just the two of us, and that she relied on me alone for pretty much everything. Still, if she hired someone else I'd probably get more responsibility – maybe even be allowed to interact with some of the less-important clients as a consultant myself! I was an expert at understanding Eleanor's thinking and it was clear to me that she was dead set on the new hire. I might as well try to make the best of it.

Trying to make the best of it proved to be almost impossible almost immediately.

Brandy Springfield was young — really young — 21 or so, with thick, platinum blonde hair and huge blue eyes. She looked like a grown up version of JonBenet Ramsey. Her slender hands were manicured, and shoes, both pointy and sky-high, graced her tiny feet, expertly matching the Juicy Couture bag whose handle looped her forearm. Her pencil skirt and silk shirt seemed conservative and appropriate for the office, but the way she wore them, was anything but

— they clung to her annoyingly perfect curves.

Crap, I thought. When it came to her business, Eleanor only dealt with competent, accomplished people, super high-achievers. I could handle competent and accomplished — I fit into that category myself, after all. But I didn't think I was going to like dealing with someone that looked like Brandy and who was also competent and accomplished.

But two-thirds of my assumptions about Brandy were blown to bits on her first day at Finesse, the moment she opened those lined, glossy, pink-as-a-rosebud lips.

"How the hell do people do this every day? I set my alarm for seven-thirty . . . AM! I'm going to need, like, twenty espresso shots just to maintain. Who makes them here, anyway?"

I paused a beat — trying to digest what she'd said. This was who Eleanor wanted for her second assistant?

"You do, actually," I said at last.

She eyed me for a long moment, taking in my plain tan cords and red polo shirt, no make up, my short, straight, bobbed hair, and glasses. I dressed like Eleanor, not some ditzy fashion plate. While anyone with a brain would instantly realize that a woman like me, so similar to Eleanor in every way, must have a key role, must be important, Brandy's heart-shaped face twisted in disdain.

"Excuse me?"

"Coffee is your job. I'll show you the kitchen."

"She's such a bitch! She resents me! I have this problem all the time."

A month had gone by and Brandy had done nothing to alter my first impression of her. For some reason, however, she saw me as a sort of confidant. Most of the time after those one-sided chat sessions, my tongue stung from biting it so hard.

Brandy sighed. "Yeah. Women just seem to get bitter around me. Especially older women. They're jealous."

I was dying to say something or roll my eyes at least, but I held back. "That must be tough," I managed at last.

"Oh, it is! In college I had to drop every class taught by a woman because they'd always give me a bad grade. I get As from men. I wish Eleanor was a man. When you look like me, it's a nightmare having a woman boss."

I couldn't take it anymore, but I tried to keep the disgust out of my voice. "She hired you, didn't she? She wouldn't have done that if she had a problem with your looks. I've always thought Eleanor was a great boss. She wants things done a certain way, that's all. Listen to her and you'll learn a lot. In image consulting, there's no one better."

"That's true, I guess. For now, anyway. I'm a natural for this kind of work, even if it is behind the scenes. I tried acting myself, you know, but the casting directors kept saying my face is just too perfect. It's too distracting. The audience would forget about the

movie or play or whatever."

"Really?"

"Yeah," she continued, evidently not picking up on the scorn that had leaked into my voice. "Same thing with modeling. I'm too young. Too beautiful. No one would pay attention to the product.

"But this. . . ." She stood and actually twirled with her arms outstretched. The gauzy lavender scarf she wore fluttered, and her hair fanned in a soft platinum sheet. "It's perfect! Who better to help improve someone's image than a pretty girl like me? What could be more positive for someone, than to be attached to this face? Associated with me? I was so excited when Daddy told me I had the job!

"But I don't know now. . . . Eleanor doesn't let me do anything important. Coffee, errands, making copies. What a waste! I should be handling clients. Justin Johnstone, for example. I could totally solve his image problem — I know it!"

I was too nauseated to respond.

"Get along with her." Eleanor kept telling me. "It'll pay off." I prided myself on knowing Eleanor, and I'd never disagreed with her before, but it was hard to trust her about Brandy. Why on earth had she hired someone so dumb and shallow? And why did she keep her on? I tossed it around my mind during the commute home, trying to puzzle out Eleanor's rationale.

". . . Daddy told me I had the job," Brandy had said. What a spoiled-brat thing to say!

Wait a minute . . . Brandy is a spoiled brat! What if her rich father pressured Eleanor somehow so that she'd give his nitwit of a daughter a job at Finesse, as a favor to him? But wouldn't Eleanor come to me for help? Maybe she was trying to protect me, which was typical of her. I didn't need protection, however. I was this close to taking matters into my own hands and coming up with a plan to rid Finesse Image Consulting of its second assistant.

In fact, the more I thought about it, the more I realized that my boss could be subtly telling me to do something about Brandy. Eleanor and I were completely in-sync, after all. She must want me to get along with Brandy so the stuck-up airhead would trust me and then it'd be easier for me to . . . do whatever needed to be done. I wasn't quite ready to act yet, however. First I needed to be sure I'd assessed the situation correctly.

"She's not ideal, but I'll make it work. Yes! You don't need to keep calling me about this, in fact I'd prefer it if you didn't. I know what I'm doing!"

Eleanor's thick eyebrows furrowed to see me standing in the doorway to her office, but then she seemed to catch herself and waved me in with her normal unflappable expression. She disconnected, set the phone down, and folded her hands on her desk.

"Sorry about that, Beth. Just trouble with my new . . . housekeeper. The agency," she waved in the direction of the phone, "wanted to know if they should send a replacement."

"Do you want me to talk to them about it?"

"No, no. Everything's fine. I need you to keep on with what you're doing online. It's definitely making a difference in the public's view of Mister Johnstone."

"Good. Uh, Eleanor. I wanted to talk to you about Brandy. She didn't show up today. That's the fourth time this month."

"You think I should let her go?"

"Well, she doesn't seem up to Finesse's usual standards."

"I can see why you'd believe that." She paused to scowl at the phone. "But there's more going on here than you know. Unfortunately, I can't terminate her just yet. There's something I have to work out first. Besides, you can handle her. I'm not worried! You won't let this affect Finesse negatively. I can always count on you to give your all for me and our clients."

Basking in the glow of her praise, I thought I understood the message behind her words. There was just one more thing I had to check.

Five minutes later when Eleanor went down to the coffee house on the first floor of the building, I snatched her phone from her desk, looked up the most recent call received, and wrote down the number.

Then I Googled it.

James L. Springfield. Springfield — just like Brandy! Was it simply a coincidence that the contact at the housekeeping agency had the same last name?

I doubted it.

I surfed further and verified that James. L. Springfield's daughter was Eleanor's second assistant. What surprised me was that he wasn't rich and powerful. He couldn't be a friend needing a favor. So why would Eleanor hire her? I then found he'd done time five years ago for extortion, and the final link in the chain snapped into place.

Brandy's dad was blackmailing Eleanor somehow. He was threatening her so that his pretty daughter could work for Finesse. I wondered what hold he might have over Eleanor, but decided it didn't matter. I knew all of Eleanor's passwords, and could access her email, her phone, even her online banking. But I never did, unless it was absolutely necessary. In this case, it wasn't. I didn't need to know how Brandy's dad was blackmailing Eleanor — what I had to do was figure out how to stop him.

The answer came to me almost immediately. If there were no Brandy, there'd be no reason for him to continue with his threats. Eleanor wouldn't have to worry about firing her; there'd be no one alive to fire. I had to admit, my conscience twinged a bit. But I pushed it aside. Brandy was conceited, obnoxious and self-centered. The world would be a much better place without her.

I had the Glock.

I could use lethal force at will.

The next week Justin Johnstone began filming a behind-the-scenes documentary for his upcoming concert tour. Eleanor wanted to be there, at least at the beginning, so she could see how to effectively promote the documentary, plus offer her advice on how to present Justin in the best possible light. No animals on the set, for one thing.

Usually, Eleanor didn't need an assistant for something like this. But Justin Johnstone liked to use street dancers on his tours and was going to film himself auditioning them in their own neighborhood — a run down, dangerous part of town — the ideal place for Brandy to meet with an accident. I'd get her alone in an alley somewhere and hit her on the head with the Glock when her back was turned (shooting would be too noisy). Then I'd take her purse, and everyone would think she'd been mugged. Perfect!

First I had to convince Eleanor to bring us both along. I told her it'd be the ideal opportunity to post pictures of the filming in Justin's Twitter feed, and Brandy could run errands, etc. Being so keyed in with Eleanor's thought process, I had no trouble making it seem like our presence on the shoot was her idea, always the best approach with Eleanor who liked to think she called the shots.

As Brandy and I drove down to the neighborhood near USC where the filming was to take place, she chattered non-stop about the commotion her presence was sure to cause on the set.

"Everyone's going to think that I should be in the movie, I'm sure. I suggested it to Eleanor. Don't you think I would make it all seem more wholesome and appealing? That's exactly what Justin Johnstone needs! Of course Eleanor said no. She's so jealous, it's disgusting! It's really just sad what happens to older women when they're around pretty girls. But I can't help it! Maybe Justin Johnstone will ask me himself. There's no way she can stop me then!"

I tuned her out, for the most part. I was too busy fingering the Glock in my bag and trying to decide whether to hit her in the temple or on the back of the neck, on her vulnerable brain stem. Bashing in that perfect face would be so satisfying! But I wasn't jealous. I was doing what Eleanor wanted me to do. Brain stem, then. More likely to be fatal in one blow.

An hour later, Brandy was in the alley. I'd told her to go that way to get to the car to fetch Eleanor's laptop, and idiot that she was, she complied. I crouched behind a Dumpster to wait, the Glock heavy and reassuring in my hand, but before she came close enough, a slim figure stepped out of a doorway across from me and got to her first.

Brandy jumped, squeaked, then relaxed. "Eleanor! You scared me! Did I forget something?"

Eleanor didn't say anything, just grabbed a hold of Brandy's bare shoulder and brought the side of her hand down, so hard and fast I could barely see it, against the back of Brandy's head. An instant later, Brandy crumpled to the ground. Eleanor supported her so that she fell gently, her perfect face turned in my direction, eyes blank, staring and lifeless.

My mouth went dry. Impossible! I thought Eleanor trusted me to take care of this for her.

She waved at me. "Beth, it's okay, you can come

out."

I rose and stumbled forward, the Glock practically dragging on the pavement it weighed so much.

"Eleanor? What did you just do?"

"I killed Brandy, of course." She knelt next to the girl and picked up her wrist. "Almost killed her. There's barely a pulse. She won't last much longer, though. I told you I'd terminate her when the time was right."

"I thought you meant you'd fire her once her father stopped blackmailing you!"

"James?" She laughed. "We go way back. This was his idea. He asked me to hire her as a favor."

My heart beat huge and fast. "I don't understand. You practically told me to kill her for you!"

"I certainly did not. This isn't the kind of thing I'd trust to an assistant."

Oh how that stung!

"Well, if you hired her as a favor to a friend, why kill her?"

"That pretty face she's always blathering on about. It's going to help Justin Johnstone redeem himself. Sure his chimp attacked Chelsey Sullivan, but the Pop Prince is going to pay for her to have a face transplant. With Brandy's face! That's all the sheeple of the world will be told. Mister Johnstone is also going to pay James for providing the perfect face, and me for making it all possible! Of course that part of the story stays with us." She chuckled again.

I crouched low, bowled over by the weight of my mis-perceptions, trying to catch my breath. It felt like gravity had reversed itself, and what I'd always thought was up was really down.

A moment later Eleanor sunk next to me, her cool, gloved hand on the back of my neck.

"I know this is tough for you. You're always so sure that you know everything about me and Finesse. You don't, clearly, but I appreciate the loyalty and that you would kill to help me. You've been the best assistant I've ever had, Beth, no question. It's going to be tough to replace you."

"Replace me?"

"Unfortunate for you, but fortuitous for me. One thing that I haven't managed to teach you is the value of capitalizing on an opportunity. Diverging from your so-carefully-constructed plan when a better path presents itself. If Brandy was the only assistant found in this alley, it could look suspicious. Maybe someone would realize she'd been killed for her face. We can't have that. But with you here too, who would ever guess the truth? No one would kill you for your face."

So fast I couldn't see it coming, she slammed a fist into my abdomen. I collapsed onto my imperfect face and fought to pull some air into my now empty lungs.

Eleanor strolled back to Brandy, picked up her purse, pulled the bills from her wallet, tucked them into her pocket, and scattered everything else on the pavement. Then she came back to me and did the same thing with the contents of my bag. By the time she was finished I could almost breathe again and I struggled to get to my feet.

My legs wouldn't work.

I opened my mouth, but no sound came out.

"Two girls who happen to work for me robbed and killed while on the job. So tragic." Eleanor wore a heartbroken expression that I knew was totally contrived like the one she'd use later during the inevitable interviews.

"How wonderful that something good can spring forth from tragedy!"

I blinked at her in disbelief. "Eleanor?" I managed at last. But she didn't say anything. She tore the Glock from my hand, brandished it in my face for a moment, then reared back. With a whoosh of air, something hard and cold smashed into my temple, and everything I knew disappeared.

R. E. CHAMBLISS is a writer, audiobook narrator, and voice actress. Her highly-rated novel, Dreaming of Deliverance, can be found in print, as an ebook, and in audio. She spends her time juggling multiple writing and voice work projects, along with shuttling her two school-aged kids to various activities. Find out more about her at www.REChambliss.com.

her pristine demise

BY AMITY GREEN
HorrorAddicts.net Episode #63

*T*he irony of bringing drinks that cost as much as twenty British pounds to men in thousand pound suits on a silver serving tray in a "gentleman's club" still hit me hard every night when I punched in for my shift – a strip joint would always be just that, no matter how neatly it was wrapped with a title, money, or even silver. It was my night to serve, rather than to dance.

Although, as one may think that would mean wearing more comfortable shoes, it did not. I still strapped my dainty, painted feet into clunky heels that expanded my lanky frame to equal the height of most patrons every shift, dancing or otherwise. A black lacy corset that made much of my cleavage, and tips as well, was matched with a sheer black thong and similar thigh high stockings to complete my attire that night. I felt as though I was dressed perfectly to match my mood. The darker, the better. It had been my motto for a few years.

My night began as most. I gobbled down a stolen handful of garnish from the bar as I made my way to the lockers, punched in, and checked the floor to get a feel of my section for the night. Nothing seemed off. Being that it was only nine-thirty on a midsummer night in London meant ambient lighting shone

through the front entrance each time the door swung open. Business would pick up after darkness provided masks for the gentlemen as they entered. My section would be one of the busiest when that happened.

For now, a mere two tables held live bodies close to the center stage where a topless girl slowly gyrated against a dingy pole, likely in tune to the sensation that she danced much faster than she was actually moving in her cocaine induced euphoria. I understood her choice with crystalline understanding. We all had our crutches.

The song ended, signaling a new girl to burst from the thick, black curtain. The topless girl pulled the bills from the hip straps of her thong then went to her knees to scrape up tips from the floor. She turned her bare bottom toward the tables as she went along, hoping to gather a few pound notes.

"Cheers, Skylar," a refreshing masculine voice said, pulling my attention from the floor.

I turned toward the bar to find Carey, the bartender I considered to be a male version of my emotionally bankrupt self, pouring two drams of well whiskey and motioning me over. We downed the shots silently, concluding our nightly ritual with light conversation about how much rain fell, or some similar small talk that we used to avoid injecting any reality into our "close-from-afar" relationship.

I thought Carey was beautiful. He was olive-skinned with a slightly thick swimmer's build and dishwater bangs that fell over hazel eyes. He had a full, pouty lower lip that curled slightly to one side when he smiled, which was just as large a rarity for him

58

as it was for me. His smile never failed to captivate my attention during the fleeting moments he allowed himself to seem visibly pleased. I could look at him for hours on end if he allowed me to.

Sadly for me, the other reason the club employed him was the fact that he knew how to keep order amongst inebriated patrons. I'd seen Carey take a rare beating; although, I'd seen him deliver many more to some of the most hulking, obnoxious of men. When business picked up at night, the club scheduled its own hulks to keep order. Until then, while business was slow, and because the club was too cheap to worry, it was up to Carey and us girls to look out for one another against the few patrons that frequented the club during daylight hours.

"It's that time," I said, both to break my reverie and to force myself onto the floor to check in with my tables. Carey handed a serving tray over the bar and set a couple drinks aboard that were meant for a previous order. I steeled myself for what was to come, and was off to work. One man groped me and I just may have chewed his arm off.

My anger induced motivation to have a grope-free shift was cut short as I approached my first table of the night. A lone man sat facing the center stage, an oddly familiar look of disgust on his face as he watched the dancer there. He deepened his sneer, tucking his jaw against two stubbly double chins. I slowed my pace as it occurred to me that I knew the man.

I stopped moving toward his table, feeling my tray begin to tremble, the ice in the drink clinking

and rattling against the glass. Time stilled while I panicked inside my skin, trying to decide how to hide myself before he noticed me. Just as he turned in my direction, I found the gumption to duck my head and crouch to the floor as if I dropped something. I arose quickly, keeping my face averted.

I turned on a heel and made for the locker room, somehow managing to keep my paces even while I fought the urge to toss my silver serving tray, watered drinks and all, into the nearest bin and sprint for the door and blessed freedom from breathing kindred air with him. Silver squealed on the pitted vanity as I shoved the tray away and peered into the mirror above the row of sinks. My eyes were huge, the ice blue color reflecting the shock I felt.

Now, gratefully alone with the scent of stale urine and sex, I let myself react, the shaking of my hands and face grew into tremors that rippled my pony-tailed hair like a blonde waterfall. A solitary tear cascaded to my pale cheek, tracking mascara before I swiped it away with a quivering fingertip. A strangled sob escaped me. I gulped air to stave off the urge to vomit the two maraschino cherries and slice of orange that had been my lone, filched meal of the day. I slammed my eyes shut, the nameless man's face vivid in my mind. He'd changed the course of my entire life in about two hours' time.

Back then, I'd been amazed at the ease with which he stuffed me into his auto. One moonlit moment, I walked alongside Tottenham Court Road, just blocks, literally moments from my dormitory, and the next instant, my face banged against the window glass of the passenger seat.

Something stunned me to the point of stillness; maybe fear of losing my young life, maybe the blow to the face. More likely, a combination of both.

He was silent as he drove with one gloved hand on the wheel and the other threatening my throat with a blade. He used that blade a while later to cut away one side of my leggings for quick access. He was nothing if not efficient with his actions and, thankfully, his time. Reaching into the darkness of the dashboard, he brought into the moonlight two condoms, one green and one purple.

"Life's about choices, darling, which will it be?"

I couldn't respond. Instead, a loud sob burst from my chest.

He was careful. He ducked his head beneath the horizon line of the rear seat when headlamps turned the corner. He held a hand over my mouth. My cheek was stuck against his chest because something sticky had been dropped onto his shirt, perhaps during his last meal. After a rather explosive bout of flatulence, he used the other condom as well.

Being raped was always a fear for a girl; although, like most my age, I was sure it would never happen to me. And damn sure never would it happen that my rapist would don a rubber and smell like stale Marmite.

I used cold water from the sink to force the images from my mind. Memory had forced me to relive the worst night of my life many times, and every time, this one included, I felt fractured beyond all hope of recovery. Sometimes I tried to think up a suitable

name for him. Nothing ever stuck. His name was always "My Rapist." It worked for me because it kept my hate fresh. The word "rape" could inspire hate in most anyone.

Emotions grappled with reason as I attempted to regain composure. My knuckles whitened with tension from grasping the edge of the vanity.

"It simply isn't him," I told myself. My voice echoed as hollow as the words I spoke.

I felt impossibly chilled inside. My feet felt as though they were welded to the stone tile by inches of thick ice. I opened my eyes to glance through the dim light at my reflection once again. I froze at the image in the glass.

I appeared physically smaller somehow, perhaps thinner. Half a once perky ponytail listed sadly to the side of a tear-streaked face. A bloodied lip trembled aside a large, angry hand print that marred my face from chin to ear. Familiar, huge eyes stared back at me, shattered youth creating a hate filled vibrancy I could feel thrumming in my soul. I shivered with the girl in the mirror, rage returning from just beneath my skin. The busted lip curled with contempt.

"It's him," we said in unison.

I'd planned for this day for years, growing sick with knowing it wasn't probable that I would ever see him again, doubting my decision to avoid going to Scotland Yard so I could punish him with my own brand of justice.

After gathering myself enough to be presentable on the floor, I stalked to the bar with renewed focus. Maybe it was years of suppressed anger, maybe it was the grating need for closure; whatever the cause I seemed to walk with more purpose, to stand taller.

When Carey replaced the drinks I'd let get melted, I shot him a radiant smile that beamed back at me from the mirror behind the bar. I took my hair down to obscure a large portion of my face, smoothing it like cornsilk across my breasts. Energy thrummed through my veins. I asked Carey for one more dram of well whiskey to be placed on my tray.

When he did as I asked, I bent close and quickly emptied half the contents of a small vial into the shot. The remaining contents I formed into a thin, white rail on a black cocktail napkin. Pleased with myself, I glanced up.

Carey parted his lips on a question, but a quick, pleading shake of my head rewarded me with his silence. The two of us stood quiet, eyes locked in understanding. A girl's gotta do what a girl's gotta do, to coin one of my favorite, grossly overused, American phrases.

I hoisted my silver tray a little higher than usual, delivered the other drinks with a quick apology for taking so long, and then headed to my rapist's table.

His eyes were fixed on a half nude dancer. I gave him a quick once over, my eyes hanging up on the bulge in his rumpled trousers. I gagged silently and blinked back accompanying tears from the momentary bout of nausea, hoping my face had not paled.

"Hi," I perked. "I'm Skylar." I smiled from beneath my partial veil of hair. "The club sends some love, honey."

He turned his attention to me at the sound of my voice. When his gaze rested on my cleavage, I pulled the bow loose to allow a deep vee to form between my breasts. He smiled, accentuating his beady, too-close-together eyes.

"What do you have for me, sweetheart?" He reached to pull me closer.

When his hand grazed my thigh, gooseflesh tightened the skin. At that point I knew what it meant when someone said someone made their skin crawl, because my whole body wanted to crawl away, not just a piece of skin. I volunteered to move in close to retain his trust. I set the shot glass down and slid the napkin alongside it, careful not to upset the contents.

"Life's about choices," I purred.

He shot the doctored whiskey in a quick gulp without taking time to ponder whether he'd rather the liquor or the smooth line of coke. I smiled again. He slid the napkin close and snorted the line with the practiced grace of a daily user. True to form, he'd used both.

I dropped into his lap, straddling him, his erection firmly ensconced between my legs. It was a posture that promised a lap dance. Instead of beginning to move my hips, I pulled the hair from my face and tucked it behind my ears, watching his face for a reaction.

His eyes widened as recognition dawned like a red sun across his features. His erection softened fast as a chemical reaction.

Adrenaline surged through my veins making me feel as though lightning could flow from my fingertips.

He sat in a pale-faced trance, stunned, wide-eyed. I couldn't help the urge to laugh.

I shifted my weight and shoved a hand deep into the pocket of his trousers, closing my fingers around a key chain and his wallet. I dropped the wallet on the table but holstered his keys deep between my breasts.

"You have a little something here," I said, motioning to the area just under his nose.

Without much thought he brushed at his upper lip, stilling his hand at the sight of dark blood staining his skin. His jaw worked frantically to make words that would never come.

I needed to act fast before he could react.

"Let go of me!" I shrieked. I shook my head back and forth feigning an attempt to get away from my unwilling attacker. My hair became tangled around us, obscuring our struggle in the dim lighting; him trying to get away from me and me doing my best to create a scene of chaos. Blood bubbled from his nose as he tried to disentangle himself from me. I made as if trying to stand and back away.

As if on cue, Carey appeared and drove a fist hard into my rapist's nose, knocking him and his chair to the floor. Some of my hair snapped under his weight but I felt no pain, only exhilaration.

Carey jerked him up by his shirt and moved him toward the door so our tussle would disturb as few patrons as possible.

My rapist stumbled. I marveled at the brilliance of my actions. He appeared to be drunk. It was obvious to no one that he bled out internally as he wobbled

out the door on his own two feet.

I turned toward the lockers in back.

"You all right?" Carey asked, seconds later as I gathered my purse.

"Just a bit shaken," I replied. "I'll call you in the morning. I need to get some rest."

"I'll get you a cab–"

"I'm fine. I can get myself home. But thank you, Carey." I looked closely at him and felt a twinge of guilt.

He was genuinely worried, had bought the whole scenario thinking I was being attacked. I pulled him into an embrace, taking a moment to inhale his scent.

Hopefully, sometime soon, I would be able to tell him my whole story in completion now that it had an ending. I broke the embrace quickly and headed out the back door into the alleyway.

Making sure I wasn't being watched, I walked to the street, where I saw a lone, staggering figure silhouetted against gas lights in the gloaming. I slid my hands into black leather gloves while I waited just long enough to see which of the parked cars was his.

When he was within reach of the door, I was there to unlock it for him. I mercilessly stuffed his bloated, unsteady body into the back seat so I could drive.

Once behind the wheel, I sat for just a moment to take in the cockpit of the automobile. The Aston Martin purred to life, gauges tilting each time I revved the engine. The car crouched at the ready, flexing in time to my foot on the accelerator.

"A prick rapist like you doesn't deserve to touch something so precious," I told him in the rear-view

66

mirror.

We stared at each other in the reflection as he fell into a bloody coughing fit that made his eyes roll toward the headliner of the car. Hissing sounds poured over his blotchy tongue as fluid splattered, mottled red against the window beside him.

I adjusted the mirror so I could continue to watch the man lose his gruesome struggle against my cocktail of drain opener and arsenic.

Ventricular arrhythmia leading to complete atrioventricular block. It was a beautiful thing when used appropriately. When my mum had begun taking the drug, Trisenox, as treatment for Leukemia years ago, the side effects of using arsenic to treat cancer were the stuff of both our nightmares. My mother passed away, leaving behind an emotionally fractured daughter, some ratty furniture, some even rattier clothing, and a half-year's supply of her meds. I'd ferreted them away.

Then one dark, predawn morning after my unfortunate meeting with my rapist, I'd awoke darkened to black at heart, crumpled and bleeding in the doorway of an electronics shop on Tottenham Court Road.

Later that day, I'd emptied syringes one by one into a bed of drain opener, then baked the mixture down for hours to form a lethal dose of heart stopping arsenic, hoping one day to encounter my rapist; too fearful to go looking for him. Instead, I kept paying my tuition by taking on work at the only thing I felt I was good for.

That's when I'd met Carey.

67

I dropped school at the end of that semester. Being raped can transform a once shining, hopeful young woman into a sad existence. I'd retained one hope, and that was to one day cross paths with the man who'd ruined my life.

At that one, still moment in time, I felt strong enough to do anything I wanted or needed. I felt Dark Skylar begin to wither, leaving room for the real me to emerge from the dying, shriveled limbs of ruined youth. Somewhere, within the root of my being, the girl I was meant to be still lived. And it was time to come out of hiding, time to start living again. As for my dark counterpart, it would figure her pristine demise would rest within his.

I kicked off my heels and shoved them into my bag, replacing them with the walking shoes I kept to wear on the way home. The Aston Martin screamed into a tight one-eighty on the dew slick surface of the cut stone road. I knew he was dead on the bench seat behind me as I turned onto the road toward the Thames.

I drove up river until full night engulfed the road when I turned off the headlamps. The river was black in its bed, roaring beside the road as I made my way toward a concrete rubbish barge dock. It was the only place I knew where the low concrete met the water, and where my deed would be hidden to passersby.

I turned off the headlamps and released the Aston Martin to roll down the embankment. The Thames ran deep and quiet here, and the drowning auto made nearly no noise at all above the din of the barges being piled high with London's rubbish nearby. Once the

68

rear bumper was swallowed by the black water, the Aston Martin was gone from sight, my rapist sealed within.

I walked back toward the lights of London with renewed intentions of sleeping for a while, showering and perhaps wearing my favorite pink and white dress, and catching the Tube to campus. I only looked behind me once. Pity, I thought. Mayhap I should have kept the Aston. . . .

AMITY GREEN lives in the town Colorado Springs, close to the mountains. She is a member of the Colorado Springs Fiction Writer's Group, and writes in several genres; her favorites being psychological horror, paranormal romance and urban fantasy. A student of Creative Writing, British Literature and Theatre, Amity has toured London and Stratford-on-Avon to enrich her knowledge of British Literature and theatre. While there, he attended workshops and several plays at amazing playhouses and theatre companies. Amity is a Colorado native and a collector of antiquities. She is a devoted mom and a lover of gardens, animals and music. To find out more about Amity, go to: www.AmityGreen.net.

Santa Claws

BY MICHELLE ROGER
WICKED WOMEN WRITERS CREATOR

HorrorAddicts.net Episode #13

"Wassail punch?"

"Check," said Elderby.

"Employee gifts as well as the family bonus checks ready?" asked Abigail Claus, smoothing her fur-trimmed evening gown in the mirror.

"Check . . . check," replied Elderby, continuing to make his way down the list. "That should be the last of it."

Mrs. Claus cleared her throat and looked sternly at her personal assistant. "Did you check it twice?"

"Wouldn't be head elf for two hundred and eleven years if I hadn't."

Her stern look quickly changed to one of a beaming, pearly white smile. "Good."

A crackle came over Elderby's head set. Faint chatter floated like a snowflake in the air as he looked to Mrs. Claus with the anticipation befitting opening night at the theater. "He's here!"

A rush of activity and excitement swarmed the Great Hall as the news of Santa's arrival spread through the staff grapevine. "He's here! He's back!" was the announcement as the elves from every department shut off their office and workshop lights and joined in the moving throng to the entrance of

the Great Hall where the sleigh was due to arrive at any minute.

Abigail Claus checked herself in a mirror one last time. She applied her usual bright red lipstick and smoothed the curls of her platinum blonde hair. She sighed and then, in a few short glides of her long legs, found her place at the red carpet where Santa was scheduled to step out of his sleigh and kiss her on her rosy cheek, kicking off the Christmas party for the North Pole staff.

A swirling red light spun in its globe indicating that the sleigh had touched down on the landing pad. Cheers from the elfin staff rang out. "Here Comes Santa Claus," in big band style, tumbled out over the crowd via the surround sound. Some elves, who had already snuck cups of the Christmas wassail early on joined in by singing the chorus. Fits of laughter broke out.

The sleigh platform descended from the roof and another cheer rang out as Santa came into sight. Elderby squinted as he waited for his cue. When it didn't come, he shot a nervous glance over at Mrs. Claus. More crackling over the headset sent Elderby's heart racing. "I know. I know. He's not waving. I don't know when to release the one thousand golden bags of snowflakes," he whispered back into his microphone.

Abigail Claus shot Elderby an angry look over her shoulder. She approached the descending platform with smiles and waves to a cheering crowd, in the spirit of Christmas perfection. As the runners of the sleigh hit the ground, her eyes bulged at the contents inside. "Hit the snow! Hit the snow!" she shouted through a fake smile.

Elderby, on command, hit the green sparkling button. A tiny blizzard of magical snow fell on the zealous crowd drunk with happiness.

When the snow cleared, Santa and Mrs. Claus were gone.

The voice of Elderby cut into the holiday play list. "Christmas bonuses are now available for everyone. Please proceed to the banquet room where dinner and your envelopes are waiting."

Another cheer rang out and the tragedy was successfully concealed.

Abigail Claus bit her last remaining nail as she peered through the frosted glass in their nutcracker-shaped bedroom door. The doctor had been running tests all night. All Santa kept repeating, as she and the security staff had whisked him from the sleigh, was, "Add Robby Willson to the Naughty list! Add Robby Willson to the Naughty list!"

Elderby cleared his throat quietly, letting Mrs. Claus know he'd returned with more information. "There's nothing in the black box. It's as if he had a smooth trip the whole night. Trajectory was good. No storms. No accidents. Not even a log entry about the police chasing him for once."

"Keep checking," Abigail barked through her tears. "There has to be some explanation! What could do all that to him?" She tried to pull herself together

as tears smeared her mascara down to her chin.

Elderby sighed. "What should I tell the staff?" he asked, trying to keep his mind on task.

"Nothing," snapped Abigail. "No one can know. He's going to be fine. He's just. . . ."

The creaking of the bedroom door interrupted Abigail as the doctor came in and sat down on an overstuffed ottoman.

""He's getting worse. The fur has nearly completely covered his body. I can still only find the two puncture marks on his hand, which doesn't explain all the blood we found on the floor of the sleigh." The doctor rubbed his bloodshot eyes and then looked up at Santa's wife. "There's more and I'm not sure that you want to hear it."

"More? What more?" Abigail asked as if she might snap from the stress. "His breathing. It's more of a growl now. At first, I thought it was a rare case of Lycanthropy. But all of the tests suggest only one other more highly improbable conclusion."

"What do you mean?" Elderby may have been hundreds of years old, but when it came to his devotion to Santa, his face was that of a small child.

"Blood samples, hair analysis, genetic testing, saliva and urine, they all point to one prognosis – cynocephaly." The doctor cringed. Abigail and Elderby stared blankly back at him. "The condition attributed to the Dog-Headed people who feast on raw flesh." The doctor took Abigail's hand. "In mythology, the same people were called werewolves."

Abigail jerked her hand away. "You can't be serious!" She laughed. Are you telling me that instead

74

of a doctor, my Santa needs a vet?" She was laughing and shouting all at once. Elderby closed the door tighter than before, hoping to keep the secret intact.

The doctor, annoyed with the fact that anyone dare question his authority stood up, dropping Abigail's hand in disdain. "You needn't worry, Abigail. I've called in an expert."

And somewhere from in the gasping chest of the old man in the bed came the faint sound of howling.

"In here! In here!" shouted Elderby, tugging Dr. Greg by the hand, as his tiny voice tried to carry over the blades of the departing helicopter. The two ran from the helipad, typically used for Santa's sleigh, and down the hall into the kitchen. Elderby knocked twice on the stainless steel doors.

"What's the password?" came a small voice from the other side.

"Reindeer poop." The doors quickly opened and Dr. Greg found himself locked into a small room with hundreds of desperate faces staring up at him.

"Any word where he's at right now?" Elderby's voice held complete authority. He went over to the group of laptop computers and put on his head set. "The vet is here," he announced. "Sound off and check in."

Half a dozen small video link boxes came up on Elderby's screen. Dr. Greg stood over Elderby's shoulder as the reports came in.

"This is Amaryllis," sobbed a small female elf. "Santa just ate two cookie makers from the bakery. I tried to stop him! Last I saw, he was headed down to the doll workshop."

Elderby clicked on another screen. "Victoria, report in!" shouted Elderby. A small crowd of elves gathered around the laptop. Crackling sounds and digital snow filled the video screen.

"Bump up the audio, Sam," directed Elderby. The sound of clicking keys from another laptop soon produced results. It proved to be a connection with terror. Victoria was begging when the audio link cleared.

"Santa, please. You don't want to do this. We're your family." She sobbed. A growl thundered through the rows of computer speakers sitting on the table. Some of the elves who had gathered covered their ears. A loud bark rumbled through the sub-woofers and Victoria began screaming. First came the awful crunch, as her tiny bones cracked and broke under the wolf's powerful jaws. Next was the gurgling and choking, as Victoria's tiny lungs filled with blood.

"It's nearly over," remarked Dr. Greg, coolly, as the others wavered in nauseated terror. Lastly, came the sound of something solid, filled with liquid bursting open under immense pressure.

"Ah, he's decided to eat the head as well," noted Dr. Greg scientifically. Small flecks of blood and brain splattered onto the camera lens, leaving crimson and grey trails as they slid down. Two elves fainted on the floor next to Elderby.

"He's acting exactly as a young werewolf! I wasn't

sure considering Santa's centuries of life. I guess you can teach an old dog new tricks!" Greg cheerfully remarked to the ghostly pale Elderby. "Can you pinpoint his location to about one hundred meters?"

"I can try," said Elderby "but I've no way of watching him save the reports from the field."

"That's just giving him a living buffet. You don't have security cameras?" Greg asked as he walked towards his large black duffel bag.

"What about the Naughty and Nice cameras?" asked Sam from across the table. "We have always used them on the kids, but why not try it in our own shops? They're radio controlled. I can program them all right from this laptop." Sam began typing furiously at his keyboard. Several small screens came on line, pumping and gyrating as they proceeded to each department inside of Santa's vast workshop.

"Why does the screen move like that?" asked Greg as he assembled the rifle from the pieces in his bag.

"They're walking," said Sam.

"The cameras are walking?" Greg was confused and intrigued.

Sam smiled wickedly, as he sent a command to one of the cameras. The movement stopped abruptly. The screen came up to show the viewer in the camera. Three dozen green and red clad elf dolls, with their eyes dark and blank, reached out as they shuffled ahead in zombie fashion.

Greg leaned in to see.

The face of the nearby Naughty and Nice elf stared back at him, its disfigured clown-like grin carved into its contorted face. Two black caverns for eyes, where

he assumed the cameras sat, stared lifelessly back at him.

Greg shivered.

"Now you know why children are especially good at Christmas," chuckled Sam. "Parents set these beauties out in different places each night leading up 'til Christmas. Check this out!" Sam sent a command to the second elf camera. The wicked little imp stalked closer to the screen.

"Hee, hee, hee," it giggled ghoulishly, making Greg's skin crawl.

He jumped back.

Sam laughed to himself and explained, "That nasty one is the upgrade for the teenagers with piercings! Every year we get more and more requests from parents for the, "Evil Cam."

Greg looked on as the zombie-like dolls came to life and sat down on shelves, chairs and window sills of all the separate workshops.

"We're set," announced Sam. "There he is!"

"Krieg!" gasped Sam. Krieg, the elfin beer maker stood trembling before the immense, grey wolf.

Greg whispered in Elderby's ear. "If you can, direct your friend to try to distract Santa until I get there."

The whole room of elves, assembled in the kitchen, gathered around the table of computers. They stood in horror at the thought of the Belgium brew-master meeting his demise.

Krieg was popular with everyone. "Who will make the beer?" was whispered around the room.

Greg rustled through his bag and found his hat,

his long coat and his surgical gloves. Elderby looked on curiously as Greg transformed from common jean clad vet to urban cowboy. Greg smirked wickedly back. "This is bound to get messy."

As Greg made his way through the narrow corridors that lead to the basement brewery, Krieg listened to the suggestions of the kitchen elves over his earpiece.

"Look out!" shouted Elderby.

Krieg jumped under a stainless steel table in the nick of time.

The wolf was temporarily confused by the shiny refection of his own hairy face. He clawed at the mirrored stranger with his massive paws.

Krieg scampered away as the claws from the wolf ripped through the steel counter as if it were paper. He climbed nimbly up a tall stack of hops.

The room of kitchen elves sighed in relief when the wolf tried to go after him, only to fall backwards on the quicksand like surface. The hump-backed wolf, with his enormous paws, repeatedly tried to climb up the sacks but each time he fell.

Krieg laughed, in spite of himself.

Santa the Werewolf took to pacing and staring at the bags of grain instead of his prey. "What is he doing now?" Sam directed the sadistically happy elf-shaped camera to pan out for a wider view. The green-eyed wolf looked from the stacks of grain to his own talon enhanced paws and then slowly up to Krieg.

Elderby watched the wolf in the process of deduction and whispered into Krieg's ear. "When I say, jump to the overhead lamp. It's your only shot!"

The firm surface under Krieg's tiny pointed shoes suddenly gave out from under him as the wolf sliced and ripped at the base of the grain. Thousands of pounds of wheat, barley and hops spilled from their hemp sacks. He heard Elderby shout "Now!" over the ear piece but the poor little brewmaster was too stout to make the leap he needed.

The wolf raised his paw in midair, extending his claws. Krieg was skewered belly first onto the longest talon.

The elves in the kitchen screamed. Elderby called out to Dr. Greg. "Hurry, hurry! He's got Krieg!" Greg ran through the maze of tight turns and twists made for tiny feet. Elderby tried to direct him, "Sharp left, now straight, another left, right tight there! Run!"

Greg rounded on the scene where the giant grey wolf was peeling the layers of Krieg's clothing off like a child savoring the chocolate icing off of a Swiss cake roll before eating the insides.

The little elf was down to his boxers and screaming at the top of his lungs for help. The wolf eyed Greg and laughed as he tossed Krieg in the air like a piece of fluffy popcorn.

The little tubby elf tried to once again reach for the overhead lantern but missed. He fell into the gaping jaws of the wolf where the razor sharp teeth pierced his body from every angle.

Blood, mixed with drool, dripped down, thick like toffee, and oozed off of the wolf's chin. The sticky red residue clumped the fur of the wolf's chest. Greg aimed the rifle straight at the wolf's throat. The gun fired and the tranquilizer met its target. The wolf whimpered in pain and began thrashing around.

Greg was cool. He'd watched elephants and lions in Africa react much in the same way. The wolf growled low and moaned. Greg looked down at his rifle to release the magazine. A strong blow to his chest sent him flying backwards, catching him off guard and unprepared. The wolf stopped briefly to stare into Greg's eyes as he pinned the man to the cobblestone floor. Saliva oozed from the gaps in the wolf's teeth. In the goo were pieces of Krieg's flesh and coagulating blood. It smeared all over Greg's jacket. The smell of beer filled Greg's nostrils. He comforted himself in the fact that Krieg must have chugged a pint before meeting the wolf.

In an instant, the wolf was off and running down the corridor. Greg got to his feet and started after him. As he ran, he changed the magazine from tranquilizers to an ammunition cartridge. As dazzling as tinsel, nestled all snug in their magazine were six shiny, silver bullets. Giant, blood soaked claw marks lined the floor and baseboards of the hallways as Greg chased Santa the Werewolf.

A squeal came from somewhere around the next bend and Greg was forced to hurdle over the broken body of an old elf, apparently thrown across the hallway in an attempt to put some space in between the hunter and the hunted. Greg stopped to examine the elf's broken body. It was a quick death; broken neck on impact. Greg cursed to himself and ran faster. Up in the distance, a large group was forming. Greg pushed past the elves that crowded into the plush room with overstuffed cushions and velvet drapery.

An icy breeze met Greg's face as he looked on.

There on the floor, wearing a red French negligee was Abigail Claus with her throat slashed open.

"She basically choked to death on her own blood," stated the doctor, frankly. He turned her head, still attached by a thread of skin to reveal the slash was nearly completely through her neck. Her shimmering blonde hair was soaked thick and red at the roots where multiple lacerations still bled, wet and glistening. Her impeccable makeup only accentuated her large, dull, doll-like eyes. Elderby took the satin sheet from the bed and covered her perfect, mangled body.

Dr. Greg stepped over the homicide scene and looked out into the raging blizzard outside. Santa the Werewolf was nowhere to be found. Even his huge paw prints had been erased by the wind and snow. "How far do you think he can get?" asked Elderby, staring out into the blinding white.

"If we're lucky, he'll drop from the tranquilizer and freeze to death in his sleep," said Greg, flatly.

"If we're not so lucky?" Elderby shivered.

"Then we have ourselves a werewolf problem." Greg sighed. "There's a rich food supply here and he knows it."

Greg sat down on the end of the sleigh bed and ran his fingers through his hair. "I'm a vet. I never signed up for this kind of work. Africa is one thing but this. . . . This is just plain weird." He paused and sighed as he stared at the red painted toe nail of Abigail Claus sticking out from under the sheet. "I'm sorry about the girl," he added, eyes red with fatigue.

82

"Oh, her." The doctor laughed. "Her murder may have been the best gift left to anyone on Christmas, actually. She was a shallow excuse of a woman."

Elderby was still staring out into the storm as he remarked, reflectively. "Santa hated that bitch!"

Greg looked up incredulously at the elf. Elderby turned and stared childlike and happily at Greg. "A whole new career is just a sugar plum away!" He handed Greg a peppermint stick from his pocket. Greg stuck it in his mouth like a cigar. Elderby rummaged through an antique chest in the far corner of the room near the closet.

"Huh?" asked Greg as he felt Elderby plop a hat on his head. An overwhelming happiness washed over him.

"Look," negotiated Elderby, indulging in his own peppermint stick. "I need an accurate marksman in case fur-face comes back. You need a new job where euthanizing toy poodles for upper class brats isn't the core part of your day. Let's talk . . . Santa. . . ."

In the distance, a sad howling cut its way through the blinding wind and snow. All eyes in the room turned to the bedroom window.

MICHELE ROGER is the author of two horror novels titled, Dark Matter and The Conservatory. She also hosts her own podcast of short stories called "Something Wicked This Way Strums." When Michele isn't writing, she is performing as a solo harpist as well as in the ensemble "Bellissima Musica." You can find both her writing and her music at www.MicheleRoger.com.

more than kin

BY HOLLIE SNIDER
HorrorAddicts.net Episode #41

*L*ate evening sun blazed down on the battlefield, turning the world golden-orange. Gunpowder and hot steel scented the air, struggling to mask the odors of blood and bowel. Commander Stephen Popham had surrendered to the Americans after only ten minutes of vicious ambush fighting. Now, British soldiers retreated to mourn their dead, leaving the Americans to cheer their victory.

In the center of the chaos, a knight stood over a body. Winds off the lake rippled the edges of his white mantle, and light gleamed dark off blood and mud. The red cross, barely discernible through the gore, marked him as a member of the ancient order; a Knight Templar summoned for battle. Pious and bloodthirsty, Sir Godfrey had turned the tide in a battle that would have otherwise landed supply lines through Lake Ontario in the hands of the British. Under the knight's leadership and strategy, American forces suffered only two wounded. They had dealt the British forces a heavy blow, taking the lives of thirteen men and capturing over a hundred more.

"I have done as bid, witch-priest," said Sir Godfrey, grimacing at the words. "Fulfill your promise, servant of Satan."

"You are brave, Sir Knight," the witch-priest

replied. "I have need of your kind here."

Sir Godfrey surveyed the battlefield, then drew his sword.

"Kill me, and you will never return."

The knight growled, but sheathed his sword.

"Very brave," the witch-priest repeated. "Fearless, one could say."

"I am armored with faith and steel." Sir Godfrey displayed the underside of his surcoat, revealing a lining of small metal discs. Soft leather encased the edges, silencing the rounds against movement. "I fear none – man or demon, living or dead." He took a small step forward, hand on the hilt of his sword. "You should fear though, for the Wrath of God shall be on your head for calling me forth."

"I did not call you. I called for one who would bring us victory, who would preserve us from the Crown's oppression. You, your spirit, rose to the challenge, answered my call swiftly and unerringly." He met the hard gaze of the knight before him. "You have only your own free will to blame."

"Send me back, servant of Satan. I waste no more breath or time upon you, lest your lies corrupt my soul."

The witch-priest bowed then. "A promise made, a promise kept." He began the incantation to return the knight to his time and place.

From beyond the shore came a low boom. Sir Godfrey turned in time to see a puff of smoke from a retreating gunboat. A cannonball, the last stray, parting shot from the British, ripped into the witch-priest, tearing his head from his body.

Lewis Crane, witch-priest for the American militia, lay on the ground before the knight, life's blood pumping from the wound in time with his slowing heartbeat. The body twitched and writhed. Fingers flexed and heels gouged the earth. The fragile book, disguised as a Christian Bible, lay next to his outstretched hand, pages fluttering. Useless now.

An anguished roar echoed in the darkening woods, one of impotent anger from the now trapped knight.

A stick snapped behind the knight. He turned, sword sliding from the sheath.

Sir Godfrey faced a servant boy, apprentice to the witch-priest. The blade hissed against leather as the knight re-sheathed it. He took a few steps forward. "I have done as the witch-priest bid, against my will, obeying the commands of the Unclean One. Now you must return me lest my knights believe I have abandoned them."

The boy shuddered and picked up the book. He clutched it to his chest, pages cracking beneath the pressure. "I – I can't," the boy stammered. "I have not the skills of the master. I am but an apprentice, one with barely the skills to turn the weather. I cannot send a knight such as yourself across a stream, much less great time." Tattered clothes and filth covered skin belied the boy's education, far above his place in the world. He took care to speak quietly, though, as it would not do for others to overhear.

"Life in this time shall not be my punishment for following one of the Devil's order."

Ignoring the insult to his master, the boy said

simply, "Witch-priests do not die."

Sir Godfrey advanced, sword drawn.

"H-h-he." The servant boy swallowed hard, staring at the naked, bloodied blade held loose by the knight's side. "We need to find his head."

"His head is gone." Sir Godfrey pointed at the still shifting corpse, struggling to rise. "Taken by cannon shot and shattered over the hills."

"Then we need to find a new head. One with the knowledge of witchcraft."

"You were his apprentice. He taught you."

The boy nodded, slow and uncertain.

Sir Godfrey advanced on the servant boy, intentions clear in the raised sword.

The apprentice ran, clutching the book and stumbling over fleshy obstacles, dodging rocks and small bushes in the failing light. He stepped on something soft and heard a gasp of pain, but ran on, uncaring of who or what he trod upon in his hasty escape. Saliva streaked out the corners of his mouth as he breathed hard and fast. Blood pounded in his ears, and adrenaline pushed him forward. Bare feet beat against the earth and small, sharp stones cut into his flesh. Crimson smears marked his trail as the boy ran north, searching for safety and sanctuary.

Hoofbeats sounded behind him. Growing louder, ever closer. Metal hissed against leather.

Hands grabbed for branches, pushing them away. Thorns and twigs clawed at exposed skin, ripping and tearing. The boy tripped and he reached for a tree trunk, steadying his stride. He glanced up.

A cabin. Logs and stone. Smoke rising from the

chimney, lazy in the cool air. Warmth and security just a few strides away. Renewed energy surged through the boy and he shot forward.

Then the world spun. Pain flared in his neck and shoulders. Hooves in front of his eyes, followed by earth, then hooves again. Sweat dripped along his face, tickling. His hands wouldn't move, couldn't wipe the sensation away. The boy struggled to draw breath, failed. Darkness seeped in, spread across his vision.

The book, his master's tome, tumbled past. Pages tore against the earth and the spine broke as the book landed. Hope fluttered in the wind, out of reach. Black velvet settled over the boy with silent finality.

The knight dismounted, a medallion depicting a double rider on a single horse thumping against his chest. Sir Godfrey watched the boy's body. Fingers twitched in the fading light, slowing as life's blood oozed in a growing stain. After a moment, the body lay still, less than a handful of yards to the cabin.

"The witch-priest has not his own," he said, retrieving the severed head of the apprentice and picking up the book, "but perhaps yours will do." He tucked the book into a worn saddle pouch, and mounted the horse.

Sir Godfrey returned and placed the boy's head on the witch-priest's neck. Flesh stretched ragged edges to meet in an angry line. Blood seeped from the wound as it closed. The eyes opened, and stared up, then blinked slowly. The witch-priest struggled to sit up, falling back with a heavy thump against the soil. He worked his mouth, opening and closing it several

times before finding words.

"This," groaned the witch-priest, "will not work. His will is not strong enough."

The dark hair of the servant boy whitened as the knight watched. Skin thinned, stretching across sharp cheekbones, threatening to tear. Brown eyes clouded with cataracts and sank further into the sockets. Lips thinned, showing receding gums and yellowing teeth.

"You must find one of the witch-priest's bloodline." Air whistled through now-exposed nasal cavities. Bones broke through the parchment-thin skin, and blood ran, thick and viscous. Black fluid seeped from the eye sockets as the orbs ruptured. Desiccated flesh separated, papery pieces blowing away on the breeze. "One of his talents or better."

Sir Godfrey knelt next to the rapidly decaying head. "Why? Why must I bring a new head to this body?"

The corpse struggled to draw breath through the rotten neck. "Magic is trapped in this body, in this heart. Another witch will not know. It was begun here and must end here."

"How long do I have?"

"Tarrytown," it panted. "Find the church, find Abraham. He will. . . ." Fresh blood oozed, washing away the last words. Thirsty ground soaked in the fluid, spreading through the soil.

Unintelligible sounds and moans escaped the ruined lips, then the head collapsed on itself, leaving another pile of dust on the battlefield. The corpse shifted and flailed, suffering a second death. Arms and legs thumped while fingers dug and pushed into the growing patch of mud.

Disgusted, the knight picked up the body. The arms twitched and hands grabbed at him, searching in vain for purchase. Sir Godfrey slung the headless corpse over the rump of the horse and secured it. He mounted the nervous animal and urged it forward in search of a proper head.

Sir Godfrey rode toward Tarrytown, bodies littering his wake.

Rumors of a headless horseman spread as the knight tried head after head without success. Three days and nights passed as he killed. Blood darkened his once white surcoat, hiding the cross emblazoned on the chest.

The moon rose, full and fat, shining silver over the land. As the knight rounded a curve in the road, a covered bridge appeared before him, ethereal in the light. A sign proclaimed "Welcome to Tarrytown" just to the left.

Sir Godfrey rode through the bridge, his horse's hooves echoing hollowly off the wood. He slowed the pace on the other side, and studied the sleepy town. Dark houses and stores met his gaze, a well at the town's center. Off to one side sat a small church. Moonlight pooled on the sills and painted shadows on the rock walls. Flickering light shone through thick windows.

Sir Godfrey entered the church, sure in his

intentions. Though the hour was late, whale oil lamps still burned in the sanctuary, their distinctive odor permeating the air. He walked slowly, visually dissecting the church.

Waxed pews gleamed in the lamplight, wood reflecting shades of copper and gold. The seats canted forward, ensuring those who would nod off during the service were quickly found. The close placement of the rows also hinted at the discomfort that would keep one awake during sermons.

Sir Godfrey sat, noting how his knees pressed against the back of the next row. A dull pain began in the joints and leg muscles flexed to keep him from sliding forward. A feeling of restriction surrounded him, and the knight drew comfort from it. He nodded to himself and sighed in satisfaction.

A priest entered the main room through a neatly hidden side door.

The knight would never have noticed the door had not movement caught his gaze. Sir Godfrey stood and walked forward.

The man smiled. "I thought I heard someone come in. How can I be of service at this late hour?" The priest studied the man before him – sheathed sword hanging from the wide belt, dark cloak covering a once white surcoat, mud and darker fluids staining the red cross emblazoned on it – and tried to hide the anxiety creeping from his belly.

"You are the priest?"

The priest nodded. "Father Abraham Crane."

The peace Sir Godfrey had found fled. Anger and disappointment surged up. An Unclean One's family member led a church.

"I had hoped you could help me. I had not, however, planned on you serving my purpose in this manner." Sir Godfrey withdrew his sword, yellow light flickering against the steel.

Father Abraham backed away, hands held defensively. "Do not shed blood in the house of God."

Sir Godfrey advanced. "If you are of the Cranes, then this no House of God, for your bloodline has defiled it."

The priest fell to his knees, hand clasped in prayer. "Our Father," he began.

"Your prayers, your false act of piety, shall not save you from damnation."

The sword cut clean and blood spattered the front pew. Head and body separated, slumping to the polished floor.

Sir Godfrey picked up the head, looking at the face. The eyes blinked slowly, once, then twice before the lids froze in death. Lips and gums paled as blood left them, and the jaw hung slack. He set the head on the altar and picked up a lamp. Sir Godfrey tilted it, watching the whale oil slide in the glass reservoir. Then he smashed the lamp against the front pew.

Bits of glass flew and burning oil ate at the wood. Flame devoured the new source of fuel. A faint scent of honey rose up as beeswax melted.

Sir Godfrey snatched the priest's head by the hair and stalked out. He trusted fire would cleanse the desecrated building of the evil housed within.

The body shifted and overbalanced the knight as he freed the bonds securing it to the horse's rump.

Sir Godfrey dropped the thrashing weight, landing a solid kick to the abomination's ribs. Trapped air left the body as a weak hiss.

The knight grabbed the witch-priest's upraised hand, resisting the urge to crush the tightening fingers. He dragged the body farther from his horse, leaving a streak of body fluids behind. With a quick prayer to the lord God, Sir Godfrey placed the priest's head against the neck stump. He watched in a mix of disgust and fascination as the foreign parts merged to become one.

"You," the witch-priest said, "did not understand. Heads hold not the taint. Rather, they hold knowledge. This one had the name of one you needed."

"Tell me," responded Sir Godfrey. "Tell me so I may return home."

"It cannot. The name has gone to the angels, released upon his death. Only magic is stored in the heart and the blood, and his has not the taint."

Scents of rot, sweet and cloying, filled the air, overpowering the smell of burning wood and whale oil from the church. The head began to collapse even as it continued to speak. Teeth loosed in their gums, perverting the witch-priest's words. "North," it slurred. "You must continue north. Track the name."

Eyes burst in their sockets. Flesh separated from bone, sliding over one of Sir Godfrey's hands where it rested on the earth. Skeletal jaws clacked and crunched. A writhing tongue flopped in the mouth, pieces breaking off in the effort to communicate. Guttural sounds and moans issued forth, but words no longer formed.

The seam between neck and body separated. Heels drummed against wood and hands slapped at the air as the body suffered another death.

Firelight danced on the walls of the tavern. Men gathered around the tables in the large room, heads down and attention focused on the mugs in front of them. Women and children clustered in corners, away from doors and windows.

Though the tavern was full, every chair taken, silence reigned, punctuated by the occasional low voice or pop of wood. The Horseman had killed again, this time the priest of Tarrytown, and numbers brought safety. Even strangers to the area were welcomed, though locals held reservations, believing those in the common room could not be the Horseman as he traveled alone and avoided population.

In one shadow-wreathed corner sat a man, dark cloak obscuring his features. He drank from his mug of ale in small sips, listening to the low conversation from his companion. "He came from the south," said the bearded fellow. "At least that's what I heard, Mister. . . ."

"Irving," Sir Godfrey glanced around the tavern, spotting a portrait of a man wearing a powdered wig. The plaque beneath proclaimed him as George Washington. "Washington Irving," the knight said.

"Anyway, I heard he was a dark fellow, big and carrying a sword." The man scratched his beard in

thought. "But I don't rightly know. Stories say he was at the Battle of Big Sandy Creek, that his head was taken by a cannonball, and now he wanders the countryside searching for it."

"And you don't believe it?"

The man leaned back in his chair, threatening to topple it. "Nah." He waved a hand and gulped at his ale. "You might talk to Ichabod though. He's a schoolteacher, been collecting the stories. He might be able to tell you more."

"Well, it is an interesting tale," he said. " I thank you for your time." A coin thumped to the table. "Let me buy your next."

A lanky man burst through the door as Sir Godfrey stood. "The Horseman," he shouted. "The Horseman is here! His horse is outside. I saw it!"

Voices rose in panic, everyone believing they saw the Headless Horseman in their midst. Chairs and tables toppled as patrons rushed to leave the tavern.

"Ichabod," called the tavern keeper. "You fool. You've gone and scared my customers."

Sir Godfrey looked at the man in the doorway. Tall and thin, with too-large eyes and a hawkish nose. "You," he called. "You are Ichabod?"

Ichabod looked at the big man addressing him. "Yes, I am." The rail-thin man stood a little taller. "Ichabod Crane, schoolteacher and historian, at your service."

The knight smiled and approached. "Come, my friend. I have heard of you and have many questions about your stories and your Horseman."

Boot heels rang on wood planks as he strode

across the floor. Sir Godfrey wrapped a strong arm around Ichabod's thin shoulders and steered him outside.

A shrill whistle cut the air and a black steed stepped forward. A corpse, headless, lay across the horse's rump, twitching against the bonds. Fresh blood trickled from the raw neck stump, staining the horse's flanks and gleaming in the weak moonlight.

Silence settled around the tavern once more. Panicked citizens had fled and echoes of retreating hooves barely cut the night air.

Ichabod Crane stared at the horse, then looked back at the man next to him. His gaze fell on a naked blade, watching in horrid fascination as it swung toward him.

HOLLIE SNIDER is the Executive Editor for Hidden Thoughts Press and owner of Swansong Editing. Her most recent publication credit is as editor of the Live and Let Undead anthology from Twisted Library Press. Hollie is a founding member of the Colorado Springs Fiction Writer's Group, as well as a member of the Horror Writer's Association, Broad Universe, the Pikes Peak Writers, and the Wicked Women Writers. She has over 15 years of writing and freelance editing experience, has taught creative writing workshops and has written several writing-related articles. Her first novel, For the Rank of Master, is due for re-release from Wicked East Press in Summer 2012, and she has several short stories in upcoming anthologies. She lives near Colorado Springs, Colorado with her family and a multitude of neurotic animals. More info can be found at:
www.HollieSnider.com and www.SwansongEditing.com

death, like, please?

BY EMERIAN RICH
HORROR ADDICTS HOSTESS
HorrorAddicts.net Episode #32

She was a vampire, but the books didn't apply to her. She didn't burn up in the sun, she was quite found of garlic pizza, and she visited cathedrals regularly. She slept in a regular bed and only had thick velvet drapes because sometimes she liked to sleep in late.

Blood was her only vice and if it wasn't for its restorative effect on her body, she would quit cold turkey. After all, depending on where she got it, it could be quite fattening. And yes, unfortunately, she did have to worry about her figure.

To those who observed her, she was a healthy, normal, twenty-five year old white chick with a mediocre body and rather large breasts. Black didn't appeal to her as a wardrobe color choice, but she was rather found of pinks and purples. Her hair was a long, blonde jumble of curls she could never control and her eyes, well, they were a shade of brown she despised. So why would anyone suspect her of being a vampire?

"The Gift," as she had heard it called in movies, wasn't something she was infected with or granted in any particular way. She was born with the craving for blood and had fond memories of suckling her mother's breast, leaving a stained red nipple behind.

Her mother didn't mind. She was a vampire as well, raised in much the same way, with much the same looks. And no one ever threatened to take her life away.

With all this calm history, in an existence that perhaps extended longer than a mortal's, but did not ooze of particular greatness, how did the Biters find her?

It seemed a stretch, but they could have monitored her eating habits, recorded her phone calls, staked out her house, and raided her garbage can for weeks on the off chance she was one of the living dead. A much more believable scenario was one of them had seen her feed on that cute aerobics instructor three months ago.

His blood had appealed to her from the first class she attended. It was healthy and alive and fat-free. She didn't kill him. No, he was still living healthy and happy in Redondo Beach, offering himself up as scrumptious eye candy for all the gym babes to lust after. But she had taken a nibble and someone must have witnessed it.

She still dreamed of the sound of his blood pumping vigorously, merrily through her veins. For a week or so, she swore she could fly. But flying, like all other myths of her kind, was not a gift she possessed.

A sound from outside her beach condo woke her from a dream about McHottie's delicious blood.

"Ugh." The moan escaped her mouth before she glanced at the clock. 2:13 PM.

She used her drapes a lot more often recently. It wasn't due to clubbing or late night TV, but because she was hunted at night.

She had started calling them "Biters" and by now they had adopted the name as a sort of self-important title. She'd been fighting them off for weeks and although she killed dozens every night, she could not seem to overcome the hellions. Plus, their super sweet blood, filled with chocolate and soda, thickened her waistline.

At first, she tried to reason with them, to tell them the truth. She explained how she had been born with the gift and could not give it to them. They didn't believe her. She argued for hours, answering their questions patiently, even though she missed her step class and the trip to the yogurt shop after. God, how she missed her frozen gummy bears! And after all that, she'd have to run the length of the beach to work off the calories from consuming them.

She had even tried telling them lies, offering them elixirs and bottles full of red-dyed corn syrup all in hopes of deterring their need, their want, to bite her. Sure, there were a couple of dark hotties in the bunch. Maybe a Criss Angel or Trent Reznor – circa 1989 – look alike might hold her interest for a few hours, but most of the Biters were scrawny tomboys or voluptuous chicks, and that just didn't do it for her.

After awhile, they stopped being nice. They'd rush her, biting every bare space on her body, marking up her tan skin and ripping her fuchsia Danskin leotards. They were bold. They were mean.

"If you will not give us what we want, we will take it from you." And they did, draining her 'til she was weak, believing her blood would make them the

immortal beings read about in dark Gothic novels.

She would scream and bash them in the head with her water bottle or jab them in the side with her hand weights, but there were too many of them. And their will was so strong, on several occasions, she was frightened her blood had transformed them into her kind. The possibility the evil creatures they believed in would truly roam the earth, scared her. How could humans want to be that kind of monster?

After a few nights of being cornered outside the gym, she decided to change health clubs. Yes, she would miss the hottie that had started all the trouble, but there would be another. There always was.

The switch in clubs threw them off her trail for a few weeks, but they sniffed her out. She hated even the sight of them, all dressed in black, eyes lined in kohl, buckles and chains rattling as they glided down the sidewalk towards her. And there were more than before.

She put on her hot-pink sunglasses and pulled her Old Navy hoodie over her out-of-control curls, but they still spotted her. Their teeth were sharp and hurt like hell. And they were costing her a fortune in dry cleaning! They were going to pay. She didn't know how, but she had to find someway to get rid of the Biters!

Weeks into the nonsense, she finally had a plan to lose them for good. She spied a novel in a bookstore window that gave her hope in stopping them.

Vampires Must Die! called to her in a way she could not ignore. There was a picture on the front of a gothed-out street kid being staked to death by a girl in a pink cheerleader outfit. A little cliché, but so were the Biters. She read it in a bright coffee shop, sipping her caramel macchiato as the sun warmed her skin.

Finishing the book, she leaned back, a smile on her face and a warm feeling in her heart. New sight and a way to destroy the pesky gloom cookies came to her. To kill them, she would have to think as they did. To play their game, she'd have to abide by their rules.

All afternoon, she ran errands and gathered supplies. When they came this time, no one would escape to tell of her existence. Sure, she would have to move, but she was running out of gyms and paying for all the memberships was eating up her savings.

Dressed in her most awesome gym gear, a pink leotard, white leggings, and magenta hoodie, she went back to her first gym, the one where McHottie worked. He noticed her right away, an immediate grin coming to his lips. The workout was a bitch, but she hopped, twisted, and turned her way through it happily, knowing by morning, she would be free.

The club had a giant glass window looking out onto the street, but she didn't need to look over to see the hellions. She knew they were waiting for her. She took her time, talking to a few regulars in the locker room after her shower and even flirted with her favorite aerobics instructor.

"Can I come over tonight?" he asked, as she stepped into the lobby. Delighted by the prospect of fresh, healthy blood, she almost called the whole killing the Biters thing off. Glancing at the gang of wannabes outside, she sighed.

"No, not tonight. I've got a dinner party. Maybe another time." She blew him a kiss as she stepped into the cool night air.

They surrounded her, a new tall one cracking his knuckles for effect.

"Hi, guys. You know, I've decided . . . I'm finally gonna give you what you want."

Pale, untrusting faces registered her promise, looking at each other tentatively. The leader, a girl in a burgundy corset and spider web skirt, stepped forward, licking her blackened lips. "I don't believe you."

"No? Well, come on. We'll go to my place. Light some candles, rock out to some Manson, drink some of my blood wine, and then," she attempted to use her spookiest vampire voice, remembering Tom Cruise's Lestat and said, "I'll give you the Dark Gift."

They followed her, a collective shuffling, a clamor of boot heels, and jingling chains.

Tentatively entering her condo, they glanced at her pink froufrou couch and white shag carpet.

A young boy with a fishnet shirt and lip piercing lifted a glass unicorn from her bookshelf. "You live here?"

"Yes." She smiled, throwing her gym bag in the closet. "Make yourselves at home."

"As if we could," said a short gloom princess with twin black braids resting on her shoulders.

"Oh, not dark enough for you? Let me fix that." She turned down the lights and pressed play on her CD player. A ghastly tune she could hardly stand poured out of the speakers. "The manager at Hot

104

Topic turned me on to this one."

A groan emitted from several of them as they took their seats. It seemed as if they felt actual pain from exposing themselves to the brightly colored furniture.

She brought out two bottles of "vampire" wine and set them on the coffee table next to her latest copy of US magazine. "Drink up. I'll be right back."

Seven pairs of kohl-lined eyes followed her to the bedroom. As she closed the door, she heard quiet murmurs and then a change in music. Good, they were getting relaxed, feeling dominant. That was just what she wanted.

She slid open her closet and ripped open the package she had bought at the costume shop labeled "Gothic Countess." Slipping the cheap material over her head, she balked at the fit. "One size fits all, my ass." She checked her backside in the full-length wall mirror and frowned. "No more late night snacks. They go straight to my hips."

A knock at her bedroom door reminded her she had guests. "You comin' out any time soon?"

"Yes, almost done," she called cheerily. Remembering she was a Creature of the Night, she closed her eyes and tried her best Bela impersonation. "Get ready to bleed." She placed a spider web tiara atop her blonde curls and crossed her fingers. "I hope this works."

She opened the bedroom door and walked into the room, making the audience stare. Donning her meanest glare, she asked, "So, you all want to be vampires do you? You think you can handle it?"

They glanced at each other before looking to the lead girl who stepped forward. "Yes."

"Very well," she said in her best Bela voice. "You're first. Come vith me."

"Did you just say, 'Come vith me?'" The lead girl scowled, crossing her arms. The others stifled laughs.

"No. Geez, what are you? Seventeen and losing your hearing? Come on, we gotta work quick before you start sprouting gray hairs."

The lead girl rolled her eyes and followed her into the bedroom. When a few of them tried to watch from the doorway, the vampire shook her head. "No, no. I can't have you watching. You might give our secrets away." She slammed the bedroom door and turned on her prey.

"Are you serious?" the girl asked, picking up the picture of the vampire at Disneyland with Cinderella.

"Put that down!" She took the picture frame and put it in a drawer next to her white satin pj's. "Lie down!"

For the first time, the girl looked frightened. She lay down on the pink flowered bedspread, buckled boots tearing at the ruffle as she did.

Eyes narrowing, the vampire approached. As soon as she bit into her victim's neck, she tasted the same sweet blood they all had. Snickers and Cherry Coke. Why did they all have such thin figures when they stuffed themselves with junk? It made her sick! As with all her victims, the girl made no struggle at the end. She simply closed her eyes, let out one last gasp and was gone.

Wiping her mouth with the back of her sleeve,

the vampire glared at the dead girl. Serves her right for having perfect metabolism!

She rolled the girl into the closet, closing the mirrored doors behind her. Opening the bedroom door, she grinned. "Who's next?"

Despite their general lack of enthusiasm about much, the little dark children lined up like kids in the school yard, fighting over who was first.

"You," the vampire said, pointing to a short young boy wearing a dog collar.

His eyes widened as he looked around at his mates. "Bu-but, I'm fourth in line. Shadow's first. See?"

"Yeah, I'm first," the boy first in line with a blue mohawk said.

"I say who goes and I say it's you, now chop chop!"

Number four ran into the bedroom, making the others moan in protest.

"Where's Cecily?" he asked as the vampire closed the door.

"Oh, Cecily, um . . . the Gift, you know, it takes a lot out of you. She's resting."

"Where?"

A clunk from the closet gave her away.

"You put her in the closet?" His eyes bulged out further, making him look like a frog.

"In the coffin. She's resting in the coffin as you soon will be, now come, lie down."

He carefully took off his shoes and lined them up by the wall. Then he took off his jacket, exposing a seriously emaciated figure. As he began removing his pants, she stopped him.

"Just get on the bed, now."

Scrambling to the bed, he laid straight as a board, eyes squeezed shut tight and fists clenched at his sides.

She rolled her eyes and bit in. At least her feeding would allow him to relax. She wondered why so many of the dark creatures were OCD?

By the sixth victim, she was over explaining where their friends were. She didn't even care that there was a pool of blood gathering at the foot of the closet. Number five's lace dress stuck out of the mirrored slider and the vampire thought that perhaps the next one would have to go under the bed.

As number seven entered the room the vampire was so full, she could hardly breathe. Her stomach stuck out as if she was pregnant and blood covered her chin and neck.

"Oh, my, God!" Seven squealed. Just then, the closet door gave way and two of the bodies toppled out, sprawling across the white shag carpet. Seven put her hands to her face, her forehead scrunched up under her extra short black bangs. "You killed them!"

"Yes, I did. And you know, they were good at first." The vampire belched. "But all that junk food, you guys really need to cut back."

"Look at you! You're a fat pig. You can't even move!" Seven shook her head, a look of disgust on her face as she moved towards the door.

"I didn't want this you know? You and your little friends pushed, pushed, pushed until I became the monster you think I am! Do you know how many sit-ups I'm going to have to do to make up for all these calories? I mean really." The vampire belched again. "Eew. . . . What was that? Cheetos?"

Seven cried, wiping her tears with a black lace handkerchief. "They were Cecily's favorite."

The vampire spit out blood with another belch. Number seven sprinted for the door.

"Oh, no you don't. Come back here, little mini-witch." The vampire caught a leather strap hanging from the last vampire wannabe's belt.

"No! Let me go! I promise I won't tell!" Seven gripped the door frame, her skull and crossbones press-on nails popping off as she fought to stay put.

The vampire held tight, tugging at the girl's cheap vinyl shirt that stretched out as she pulled. Breathing heavy and unable to fight even the little 89-pound Lydia Deitz look-a-like, she let go.

"Fine. Forget it." The vampire panted. She felt like she had a fifty-pound weight on her chest. "Get out of here, but you better leave me alone. If I ever catch you stalking me again, I'll drink you up!"

The girl pulled away and was out the door before the vampire could change her mind.

The vampire saw number seven a few months later, but she had changed. Instead of lace and velvets, she wore a Catholic school uniform. When Seven saw her, she pulled out her rosary and mumbled a prayer.

The vampire moved anyway, just in case the teen got the bright idea to turn vigilante. She settled in a

cute beach house in Santa Barbara. She was even able to return to her old gym where McHotAss worked. However, whenever she let her desire overwhelm her, she made sure they were behind closed doors where no one could see. It just wasn't worth the calories.

EMERIAN RICH is a writer, artist, and Horror Hostess of the popular international podcast, www.HorrorAddicts. net. She is best known for her Night's Knights Vampire Series. She also writes the Sweet Dreams Musical Romance Series under the name Emmy Z. Madrigal. For more information, go to www.Emzbox.com

graveyard shift
& reshift

BY H.E. ROULO

MOST WICKED 2009

HorrorAddicts.net Episode #31

Boyd smacked his lips and sat back. "I may have to undo a button."

Meg laughed. "I'm glad you liked it." She gave him a peck as she gathered their dinner dishes, his seated position allowing her lips to meet his evenly. She moved a few steps to the sink and rinsed the chipped plates.

The vinyl chair sighed with relief as he rose. Despite his words, Boyd tucked in his flannel shirt and got his hooded jacket then checked the Budweiser clock on the wall. "You mind that we only got one meal a day together?"

"No," she called from within the refrigerator. He could barely see the top of her blonde hair over the door.

Grinning, he set his elbows on the door and leaned over to look at her. His grin faded as he saw the open lunchbox in her hands. "I hate Twinkies."

"But somehow they're always gone. Anyway, you wanted that extra big box so you gotta eat them." Meg looked up. "You ain't throwing them away?"

"I said I wouldn't," he grumbled.

Her lips turned up sweetly and her gray eyes sparkled. "I made you a special sandwich."

He mumbled his thanks, reminding himself to eat in the field rather than let Doug see the heart-shaped sandwich. He took the lunchbox and got his keys from the top of the refrigerator. Sliding a finger thoughtfully along his hand-held GPS, he tucked it into his pocket.

She inspected their small living space with a housewife's practical eye, shoved a box of cereal to the back of the counter and then bustled to the washing machine closet.

"Easy night?" she asked, stooping.

"Not much changes in a cemetery. Almost a full moon, so I suppose the vandals could come back."

She wasn't listening. "God, Boyd, I've asked you not to put your work stuff straight into the washer. I need to treat. . . ." She held up the shirt. Layers of grime and cemetery dirt overlaid the faded blue plaid. His favorite shirt.

Her pale hand folded the cloth onto itself for a better look and her fingers slipped through parallel tears in the fabric. "It has blood on it."

He took it from her hands and shoved it into the washer. "God gave me a dirty job – gruesome sometimes. You never could handle what I got to see every day. Better you don't ask for details."

"Okay," she whispered, wiping her hand off on her pants. "I'll mend it for you. What's one more?" Her eyes flickered to the pile of clothes she'd brought home from her work at the dry cleaners for alteration. Her shoulders slumped.

He stepped between her and the work, not liking the shadows under her eyes. "Want I should drop you at the movies?"

"No." The tattered fringe of lashes around her large gray eyes flickered toward him and away, "I got a feeling like there's something in the air tonight. I think I'll just turn in."

"Okay. Love you, babe." He squeezed her, not too tightly, feeling the nubbiness of her red polo shirt catch on the roughness of his calluses, as if the surface of his hands didn't want to release her. His eyes searched hers.

She reached around him and squeezed back. "You're a big and important man, Doc."

He straightened his back and swaggered to his van. As the engine coughed to life a smile spread his thick lips. Home life was good, but there was someone waiting. His eyes traveled to the faded moon. She should be just waking up.

And she'd be desperate for him.

Boyd whistled softly between the gap in his teeth, swinging his lantern and metal lunchbox in one hand and a shovel in the other. When the machinery couldn't fit between old plots, like tonight, trusty Boyd was called on to dig the trench by hand. The grass was high enough that he had to leap slightly to get to the next flat headstone. This was his third circuit of the night. *Wonder when Doug'll remember to cut the grass here. He's lazy because this section has the oldest graves and no one complains. Fine by me.*

Dirt had clumped up where the shovel's handle met the shiny metal blade. With an underhand swing he slapped his shovel against a small cherub-covered tombstone. *Can she feel the vibrations of my coming?* She'd been waiting for him a long time now. Forming his shaking hands into fists, he pushed the thought down. *It's not late enough yet. Caution.*

For lunch, Boyd sat facing heavy iron gates surrounding marble buildings inscribed with names of once important families. He gobbled his sandwich, predictably heart-shaped, in three bites and his hand searched blindly for more, wrapping around a pair of Twinkies wrapped in crinkly cellophane. He squeezed the packet until it strained from the pressure of the air within. Tossing it back into the long black lunchbox, he swallowed and snicked the lock into place.

Bowing to the largest mausoleum, Boyd wiped his mouth on the back of his sleeve. *That's enough waiting. It's time.*

A prickly stand of pale birch trees came into sight at the bottom of the hill. There were no roads this far out and the cemetery didn't consider it useful for new plots because of the mature tree roots. Boyd knew better. He slipped through branches as if they were iron gates. Hushed privacy cocooned him, stretching from the vaulted tree-limbs above to the webbed undergrowth. He'd carved his name on a branch high above. No one else might notice it, but it was there all the same.

He pulled out his GPS and circled inside the grove, counting out loud, brushing the trees as anticipation built. Breathing faster, head cocked, he set down his lunchbox and hung his lantern from a hook he'd screwed into the bottom of a low tree limb. Sometimes he brought a pulley and some extra equipment, but this time he wouldn't even need a pickaxe. He tucked the GPS away and took out his shovel, which glittered in the dim light of the lantern. The regular cry of metal against rock echoed off tombstones as Boyd's shovel bit and lifted. Bitter smelling earth formed a heap. Trained muscles bunched and stretched with mindless power until he reached the firm resilience of wood.

Boyd frowned and bit his lip, slapping the shovel down with a little extra force. With a sculptor's ease he carved dirt away from a polished wood lid, but tension tightened his shoulders. Breaking rhythm, he listened to the muffled pant of his lungs and the utter silence of the nighttime cemetery. Dread rose in a hot wave. *Something's wrong.*

His shovel thumped against the inert top of the casket a few times. Inhaling with a wet sucking sound, he spat a sweetly dirt-flavored globule onto the ground. "It's too goddamned quiet," he growled, releasing his shovel to fall onto the lid and listen. He pawed at the last of the dirt, snuffling and muttering to himself. Rising like a beast, he shook the tension out through thickly corded arms and hard calloused fingers, fighting for control.

"Just need some light." He leapt out of the hole and turned the lantern.

By the light of the lantern his shadow reached sharply over the fresh grave and scarred lid of the coffin. He flipped his shovel around so it was at the

ready. Suspecting what he'd find, Boyd slid back into the open grave. With a solid kick from one meaty leg the top half-lid of the coffin flew open. His practiced eye took everything in under the dim blue light of the lantern. His new toy was broken. Just to be sure, he pressed anxious hands against her cold skin.

His sweat and the acrid odor of the chloroform mixed with a sweet perfumed stink. She should have woken up hours ago. He smacked her cheek, just to hear the crack of skin on skin. Purple from the slap that had knocked her unconscious and let him drug her and bury her discolored otherwise pale skin. Twinkling sequins on her black party dress celebrated her death. *Thought she was a fighter. Didn't she rip my favorite shirt like a little clawed animal?*

All day he'd anticipated their night together. Sighing, he slid his arms down her body, moving them through tangled black hair and past the hem of her twisted dress, feeling rough sequins and hearing Twinkie wrappers crinkle as he dislodged them within the coffin. Hands lingering regretfully, he smoothed the layers of her short black skirt. Her sequins tinkled like bells. With a grunt, he shoved upward on the lower portion of the coffin lid. Soil that hadn't been cleared clattered like gunshots. With both sections open he could see the empty water bottles and the oxygen tank where he'd left it next to her bound knees. When he lifted the heavy green tank and tapped it with a thick fingernail a dense thunk answered. Three torn cellophane wrappers fluttered as new air filled the coffin. She'd eaten the damned Twinkies while the air around her became

116

stale with the sweet buttery stink. She'd had enough air, probably; she'd chosen not to use it. They'd hardly had any fun these last few nights. *I thought sure she'd go a few more.*

"Goddamn coward," he swore at the fresh corpse.

She smiled up at the sky, lips curved with eerie peace. Her folded hands clutched something. Sneering, he pushed them apart, expecting to find a crucifix or religious memento. Instead, a small pouch torn from the bottom layer of her cotton skirt adhered to the skin of her chest. He pulled it up with a rough skin-on-skin sucking sound. She had wound her dark hair into a drawstring for the bag. Reluctantly, he poked a thick finger into it, feeling gritty dryness. Something moved. He shuddered as a small red worm slithered from the opening. The eyeless end waved vainly in the air for somewhere to bury itself. Inside the coffin, scratches formed patterns and meaningless words along the coffin walls and curved lid.

She went mad. Crazy girl ruined my plans.

Boyd slammed both lids home then clambered out of the hole, dragging the shovel with him. He surveyed the hidden unused corner of the cemetery that he'd claimed and shivered within his sweaty t-shirt. Limbs creaked softly. A pale moth fluttered mindlessly toward him. The furry body smacked his cheek with a painless thud. He lifted a belated hand and swatted the corpulent body to the ground where it writhed in the dust and became still.

Even moths think they're better than me.

He bellowed, veins in his neck rising to the surface in mottled purple bulges, and threw the small scrap

of fabric down. A stream of powder drifted from the mouth of the pouch, identical to the dirt all around them though darker with her blood.

The small body of the moth sank beneath his grinding work boot, protected by the soft dirt. He kicked it toward the open coffin. Raging, he tore the hook from the tree limb, shaking the tree. Ragged debris rained from the birch's contorted limbs onto his neck like tears. Bits of cobweb and tiny spiders lit on his bare arms. He swiped at them and pounded his fists against his hard biceps.

Without her, I'm just the cemetery caretaker and night watchman. I'm a guy with a big light, paid on the cheap to keep kids out at night. But that's not my real job. I always knew. I do what no one else has the balls to do; I test them. And they always let me down.

A breeze raised goose bumps and he shivered, suddenly conscious that he stood with his head down, feet spread, panting like a freshly broken horse. He thrust out his jaw and adjusted his belt, glancing speculatively over the ground at the base of each of the trees and moving his lips as he counted. But shook his head, disappointed. *Sure, sometimes I can keep a couple going at once, but I haven't maintained anyone else in a while. The last one'll be way dead and stinking by now.*

I don't like to see them once they're dead.

He reached into the hole and pulled up the green tank. Rust left a dark streak on his pant leg. Something, some kind of soft sound, made the skin on the nape of his neck prickle. He turned sharply, lifting his lantern and the shovel like an ax.

118

Someone gasped.

Who'd dare watch me? Enraged, Boyd ran toward the brush with a fierce roar. He jumped the bush and trapped the crouched figure. From where she cowered on the ground, his wife's large eyes stared. She'd never been pretty, and now terror made her skin as pasty as the corpse he'd dug.

He snatched her up. "You spying on me, Meg?"

"Oh, Boyd," she sobbed, "Oh, Boyd, no. Why? I didn't want to believe it – but those missing girls in the news. . . ." Tears streaked down her cheeks and dripped onto the back of the hand that gripped her faded red cotton polo shirt. Nubbins caught against the roughness of his calloused palm. The shovel's hardness pressed between them. The blade smelled like dirt.

He slapped her for the first time.

She wrapped two tiny hands around his wrist, "I won't tell. I swear," she babbled. "Doc, no! You're important! You're big and important! You don't want this – I'm your wife!"

He pulled her close to snarl into her face. He'd been the perfect husband and she'd ruined it.

She brought her knee up. So tiny and delicate, he'd taught her that trick so she wouldn't get raped. Her knee connected and fire lit his groin into a little piece of hell. Crying out, he dropped her. She snatched the shovel before he could use it for support and ran away, opening her black purse and screaming for help.

He lunged, belly bouncing against his belt buckle and twinging pain shooting into his gut with every stride. She raced toward the open grave. He caught

her by the fabric of her shirt but she twisted so hard that the material popped out from between his fingers. She struck, flashing the knife that she'd pulled from her purse; his own kitchen knife that had probably made the sandwich in his lunchbox. The blade sliced across the inside of his forearm sending a rush of dripping blood down his arm. He roared and knocked it from her hand. Sobbing, she swung his shovel.

He dodged, bending down to pick up the metal lunchbox he'd left by the grave. In the same motion, the sharp metal corner connected with the side of her head, tearing a section of scalp loose. She spun in the air then flopped onto the ground face-down and limp. The shovel flew outside the light of the lantern swinging crazily in his left hand.

He scrambled forward and crouched next to Meg. She moaned. He grabbed the back of her head, feeling where the scalp hung like a toupee and smashed her face into the ground until she stopped moving. Sticky fingers came away covered with pale blonde hair. It was the most exciting night they'd ever spent together. He patted her head, rubbing the loose hairs off with a final wipe then picked her up.

In the distance, a light went on in the work shed.

Shaking and cursing, he extinguished his lantern. In near darkness, he jumped into the still open grave with his wife on his back. He kicked the lid open again and shoved Meg into the box. She was so tiny it barely took any adjusting to fit her. Next came the metal air tank and then he slapped the lid down. When a rapid search for his shovel failed, he squatted beside the grave and shoved dirt in with hands and feet.

Gravel crunched nearby. That meant Doug, the grounds person, walked on the gravel path that circled the regularly spaced graves of the cemetery proper. Boyd pulled out his handkerchief and wiped the corner of his lunchbox as he left the shelter of the trees. Stepping on the ancient names, he waved his lantern in greeting. Doug waved back and started toward him. Cursing, Boyd wiped one hand with the other on the handkerchief as he went to meet Doug.

"What dat noise?" Doug asked when he got close enough.

Boyd held up an arm. "Maybe you heard me. I cut my arm and screamed like a girl."

Doug laughed.

"You come out early," Boyd said.

"Couldn't sleep. Ma's out of town and I never sleep good when she's gone."

"Oh yeah? My wife's gone visiting," Boyd said, "I plan to sleep great."

"Hey man, you better come get dat cleaned."

Boyd's eyes narrowed, but then he smiled a big brown smile and wiped his arm with the handkerchief. His and his wife's blood saturated it. "Cemetery dirt ain't any worse than garden dirt."

Doug's eyes gleamed. "Just be glad it don't grow what you plant."

Boyd walked beside him and laughed like it was the funniest thing he'd heard. He sobered, "Where's the trash? I got to throw away the rest of my lunch." There was the faint crinkle of a Twinkie wrapper.

The next night, Boyd brushed his thinning hair, pulled on his favorite blue plaid shirt and headed to work. Tonight was his Friday, the last night of his work week. Dropping hints Meg might have run off was so easy that, in another couple days, even he would believe maybe she'd got fed up with their little trailer and doing alterations at the dry cleaner, and left her insensitive, grave-digging, night-shift husband.

Lantern in hand, he made his rounds. When the clock tower chimed, he went into the shed for his heavy lunchbox and sat with Doug, who was good for a laugh. The metal lunchbox gleamed from its fresh cleaning. Boyd threw open the lid, grabbing up the sandwich, and talked through it as he took hearty bites.

"Why you want to work nights?" Doug asked. He snapped his teeth on a pretzel and hard flakes dropped onto his knee. Cut grass and gasoline fumes from the heavy machinery around them flavored their lunches with a green earthiness.

Boyd heaved his shoulders. "Boss don't care when I work and the vandals were getting worse. I found I liked it." He'd liked it enough to be the vandals. He paused with his mouth full, examining the sandwich pressed between his fingers. Ragged edges made it look as if someone had hacked the crust off.

Doug peered into Boyd's open lunchbox. "Thought you didn't like Twinkies?" He lifted the cellophane package by the corner so Boyd could see it.

Boyd's pulse rose in his ears. "I didn't put that there."

Doug dropped it with a startled exclamation. "Oh, man," he laughed. "How long you had this thing? I didn't know they could get like that. I thought they embalmed with the same stuff we use."

Boyd leaned way, way down, the trip taking forever. Through the clear wrapper he could see where the golden flesh had been macerated and nubby red worms coiled in a sickly pile of pale white cream within the trapped confines of the package. They wiggled feebly.

Doug scooped it up while Boyd's hand still moved in slow motion. Doug shook it with a furious motion, sending cream and worms flying around inside. The packaging popped, gushing white pus and squirming worms across the lid of Boyd's lunchbox. Doug laughed with dismay. He turned the lunchbox upside down and shook it so that the metal lid flopped open and closed with metallic clangs. Pus dripped off in clots.

Boyd yanked on his shirtsleeve, seeing where the stuff had glommed onto the fabric. An oily shop rag took away the worst of it, leaving a streaky stain.

Doug looked up. "You're tearing your shirt. See there, the mending's coming out. Did you do that yourself? Looks like crap. Meg'd better come home soon, huh?" He looked back at the lid that swung open and closed, open and closed. "Maybe she packed your lunch before she left?"

Boyd yanked the neck of his shirt out so he could see the wandering stitches bunching the fabric over

the rents in the shoulder. *This is my favorite blue plaid, the one Meg found.*

His stomach heaved. "I got to check something." Snatching his lunchbox away from Doug, he banged out of the shed. The lunchbox fit under one arm like a football while he dashed through the field of tombstones.

As light peeked over the horizon, he saw his mausoleum, the white trunks of the birch trees standing as vivid zombies in the hazy night. Though he liked to think he was immune to the terrors of a cemetery, this night his skin crawled. Fingers of fog resisted the weak light of morning.

Boyd shook his head, trying to clear it of dread.

He passed through the trees and halted, hand to chest. A mound of soft dirt rose in the clearing as if shoved up from underneath and the corner of the coffin jutted over the top. He puffed out his cheeks, wondering how he'd left such a mess. *Jesus, I know I rushed but the thing looks nearly uncovered.* He circled the coffin but didn't touch it. After a few minutes searching, he found his shovel wedged near the grave. Giving it a grateful wet smacking kiss, he hugged it to his chest and looked once more at the gleaming wood that had erupted from the earth like some burrowing insect. Polished red wood looked wet in the faint light.

As he crept toward the coffin, blood pulsed in his ears, making hearing impossible. He leaned over the casket, which lay at an angle in the semi-filled hole. A few scoops with his arms freed the upper lid. Wiping sweat off his lip, he opened it.

He laughed. What did he expect? The two women lay intertwined, limbs locked together. Meg's head rested on the other woman's breast, her pale hair yin to the dark one's yang. Red worms already squirmed in the first corpse and a writhing bundle at the base of Meg's neck promised her turn was next. Black sequins twinkled under her bluish cheek. Boyd's laughter died. He hated looking at the dead ones.

The rising moan of a motor started in the shed.

Cursing fluently, Boyd shoved and the coffin slid. Shaking, he forced the coffin into place within the hole. *Too shallow, but I got no choice.* Loose dirt flew from shovel, fists and feet; his heart pounded and sweat dripped in rivulets. On all fours he gathered loose leaves and spread them over the grave, making it disappear into the forest floor. Bits of leaf stuck to the prickly uncut stubble on his cheeks.

Back home, he chucked his lunchbox into a Dumpster at the entrance to the trailer park. Weary feet tracked mud across the house and into the bedroom where feverish dreams left him hollow-eyed.

While the sun set in a smoky red haze, Boyd rose. Disbelieving, he pressed hands to his eyes. Breath panted as if the air was bad and gray spots shrank his vision. His boots, clean of mud, stood lined up outside the bedroom door.

Wheezing, he stumbled out the back of the house and stood next to the barbeque breathing the hot evening air. Back through the open door, Meg's sewing machine still sat on the dining room table. Her pile of mending lay next to it. He couldn't tell

– had they been finished? He pictured the slender hands that couldn't span one of his own digging into wood, splinters driving into the calluses that sewing had made on her fingertips, and sending shards under her nails. He pictured those hands breaking through and combing soft dirt. Other cold hands joined hers to dig and dig. He punched his thigh and threw out his chest, then staggered into the house.

Dressed in black, he arrived at the cemetery and went straight for the corpse. Under the secret blanket of trees, his shuttered lantern lit his mausoleum with only the faintest of sparks. As feared, the polished sharpness of a wooden corner jutted from the earth, half ejected from the crumbling mound it sat on. He stepped forward, shaking, and saw where the lid rested half-ajar. Darkness hid the contents.

"Who's doing this? Is it you, Meg?" Boyd's throat constricted.

The shovel slipped into the dark crack. Stepping closer, he pushed the lid upward. The heavy weight of the wood resisted, pressing down until he got leverage to swing the hinged piece upward with a shuddering toss. The door whumped into the dirt. As dust settled in a fine layer over the open coffin, a pale moth fluttered out. Inside the open door, his name lay scrawled into the wood so deeply that it obscured the strange etchings that had been there. Dark and pale strands of hair clumped within a sticky patch but no bodies lay within.

"Oh, God!" Boyd whimpered, clutching his shovel to his chest and swinging his head around frantically while his shoulders rose. He backed from the coffin, sobbing, desperate to run away, but the evidence of his crime hung there in the open, ready to be found.

Teeth chattering, Boyd ran forward and swung the lid shut. He tried to push the coffin back into the hole, but soft earth had collapsed into it. Blinking and snuffling, he jumped into the hole and shoveled at the loose stuff.

A woman sighed. Sequins tinkled in the breeze.

He stopped, listening so hard the skin behind his ears hurt. Only the patter of slipping dirt was audible from within the hole he'd dug. He began again even more feverishly, tossing dirt up to the grass.

Soil rained back down.

Clods of dirt pelted him from every direction. He covered his head with his arms, afraid to see who was shoveling dirt onto him.

Hiding his eyes with a bent elbow, Boyd leapt for the side of the trench. Meg waited. She stared at him with large gray eyes, like the eyes of something dead, and slammed his own shovel into his face. A haze of red flooded his vision, then blackness.

When he woke up, his head hurt but a soft pillow cushioned his cheek. He groaned and tried to press a hand to the throbbing. The sudden pull of rope against his thick wrists stopped him. Blind, the familiar hot scents of wood, fabric, dirt, and death pressed against his sanity.

The coffin lid flew open, the sudden light as revealing as a photographer's flash. Boyd lay pressed into the corner of the coffin blubbering. He had wet himself and the smell of urine stung his nose. Only one eye could see, the other one watered uselessly

where Meg had crushed it with the shovel. Meg crouched over him in the opening of the coffin lid, face dirty and hair wild.

Boyd's tears pooled on the side of his nose. "Oh, thank God! I did wrong and you wanted to punish me, but now call the police, Meg! Just call the police!"

"Dead people don't call the police, Doc." Drool dripped from her mouth and pooled along his neck. A wet squirming told him that there was something alive in with him.

"You want to punish me. I get that. But it's over now."

"You're smart, Doc. You're big and important. I do want to punish you, but I'll be fair as you. I promise if you can just last, I'll dig you back up. Think you can last?" She shoved the door shut as he tried to argue.

"I'll wait," he whispered to the coffin lid, "I'm the toughest SOB there is, and when they dig me up I'll still be waiting. She's just giving me a taste of my own medicine, thought jail'd be too good for me. She's a Christian woman."

Meg's words came through the door as the first shovel of dirt hit the lid, "I'll dig you up, probably. But it's not just my vengeance you got to face."

His bound hands clenched, touching against a twisted cotton skirt as he heard the tinkle of sequins. Screams rose in his big barrel chest. He felt the body of the dead girl shift, turning toward him in a slow roll. Twinkie wrappers crinkled and cold hands slid along him pulling at his shirt.

She leaned into him. "Will you make it last?"

There was a slight hiss as she released air from

the tank. Just a bit – rationing carefully. Her tone was smooth with promise, "Do you want to make it last? How long do we have together?"

The tone turned ragged and hoarse, "Because I can make it feel like an eternity."

The noise was terrible. But no one could hear him, there in his mausoleum, buried, just like the big and important man he was.

H. E. ROULO'S science-fiction novel, Fractured Horizon, the first Rivenspace novel, is available as a downloadable audio book at Podiobooks.com. It was a 2009 Parsec Award Finalist for Best Speculative Fiction Story (novel). Find her zombie story "The Killer with Eyes of Ice" in the Live and Let Undead anthology. H.E. Roulo's short stories have appeared in Flagship, Horror Addicts, and Podiorack Presents - Visionaries. Follow H.E. Roulo on twitter @hroulo. To find out more about H.E. Roulo, go to: www.HERoulo.com.

Wings of revenge

BY LAUREL ANNE HILL
MOST WICKED 2011
HorrorAddicts.net Episode #63

The dark mass swirled through the gray sky at dusk, like charcoal smoke riding the last winds of day. Carlotta knew that swirl, that near-silent movement of countless wings. Bats. The annual arrival of migrating bats. She swung open her white picket gate and walked toward the graveyard and derelict church at the edge of town. The funnel cloud of flying mammals fanned out from a hole in the former house of worship's peaked roof.

Well, that would show Maude and Emily Haggerty, all rotten in the ground while bats took over their precious sanctuary. While Carlotta – the woman no decent man should hold hands with – thrived.

A chill of gusty February wind stabbed Carlotta to her bones. She shivered and set her halogen lantern on the ground, the lamp's glowing elements like two blunt fangs. Time to zip shut her down-filled nylon jacket.

Odd, the way bats had returned to Pine Grove, California, already. They weren't due until March or early April. Maybe global warming had screwed up their instincts. They looked smaller than usual, too, as though from a different colony. She ought to call Professor Damian now. Bats were his research thing. She just got paid for counting them.

Carlotta fumbled through her cell phone directory and pressed the biologist's number. Three rings. An electronic greeting. Dammit, she'd forgotten his Thursday night lecture. No way he could drive to her place tonight. She'd have to investigate those batty bats who couldn't tell the difference between late winter and early spring.

"You could have warned me about the early migration," Carlotta teased in her voice mail message to Damian. "I just returned this afternoon from two thrilling weeks in Fresno. What if I'd stayed longer?"

Bar-tending stints in Fresno were never exciting. Necessary in these shitty economic times but dull as photographs of cow patties. Photos. She should snap a picture of the bats for Damian. Carlotta leaned her hiking stick against a pine and aimed her camera phone, making sure she caught the high-desert scrub as well as the five-o'clock shadow of bats above the earth's face. A few pushes of her finger sent the photograph onto a cyberspace road, or whatever path such things traveled.

She tightened the straps on her backpack. Bats had set up roost in the old church during her absence, a new location for them. There'd be fewer of the creatures hanging around in the barn beyond the graveyard. Maybe none up the hill in the cave near Jake Wilkin's secluded cabin and lab for alternative pharmacy. Carlotta gave Jake a jingle.

"I'll be up your way before dawn," she said to Jake's voice mail, "either tomorrow or the following day." Jake never answered his phone or made call-backs. That's just the way he was. A good man, Jake, for someone who brewed illegal drugs and couldn't fuck worth shit. "Bats are back," she added. "Keep out of the way while I'm counting and don't shoot me."

Shots. Tomorrow she had better make an appointment for a rabies booster and start a list of her potential bat-watching expenses. Bats devoured insects and were important crop pollinators, although in Northern California they never migrated far. Professor Damian would bring the money she required. He always did.

Not that Carlotta was an expert on bats. Mainly, she wasn't afraid of back roads and had good rapport with the local men. Not with their wives, though. Damian Haggerty left money on Carlotta's dresser and everybody in Pine Grove knew it. Money left on a bedroom dresser didn't fit most wives' description of reputable income.

The light from Carlotta's lantern caught two marble angels spattered with bird droppings. Maude and Emily Haggerty's grave markers. Those twin spinsters from Hell kept Carlotta from getting a college scholarship twenty years ago.

"No Christian morals," Maude, then a school counselor, had written in her evaluation of Carlotta's worthiness. How could that old harridan have sent such lies to the scholarship committee?

"Pine Grove High shouldn't reward a whore," Emily had whispered in all the influential ears. Hell, Damian had been the only one screwing Carlotta back then, although Jake wanted to. Damian's grandfather had been Emily's brother. Maude and Emily practically choked seeing Damian dating Carlotta,

the daughter of the town drunk. Self-righteous old biddies.

Well, Maude and Emily never would bother Carlotta again, although Damian's continuing passion for her could have made his aunts glow in the dark with fury. Lucky for her, their power over Pine Grove ended ten years ago, when their Chevy sedan skidded on black ice and carried them into the hereafter.

Good riddance.

Carlotta pushed a spiral curl of ash-blonde hair away from her face and headed toward the neighbor's barn. She might have become a professor of bats, had she received that scholarship money. Even married Professor Damian. In life, Maude and Emily Haggerty earned every splatter of bird poop they now received.

Past the graveyard, ground softened under Carlotta's hiking boots. She held her halogen lantern high and climbed over a gate. Good thing the full moon poked through the overcast. She prodded the ground with her wooden hiking stick and navigated the cow path leading toward the splintery barn.

Carlotta pulled open the barn door. A musty odor greeted her. No hint of fresh bat guano. The barn wasn't this year's main roost.

Her pocket vibrated with the arrival of a cell-phone call from Damian.

"Those aren't my bats," he said.

"They have to be yours," Carlotta said. "Where else would several thousand bats have come from? Are your research dudes on an early spring break or something?"

"I called my assistants," Damian said. "None

reported signs of early migration in any of our colonies."

"Well, tell 'em to go check again," Carlotta said, aware of the rising pitch of her voice. "The bats didn't come from Wal-Mart. Google bat news or something. See if anybody's misplaced a colony." As if anyone could accidentally lose thousands of bats.

"All right, all right," he said. "But I need to know the species. Have you had your rabies booster yet?"

"Due in a month or so."

"You should be fine," Damian said. "Sneak close enough to get a description. Just before dusk, as usual. Size, coloration, facial features. By the way, before, when you saw them, did you notice anything different?"

They'd been in the sky, not next to her. Yet they had seemed smaller than usual. Still, bats lost body weight during winter and would always appear smaller by February.

"I'll get a better look tomorrow," Carlotta said. But she couldn't afford to go on a wild bat chase for free. "Will you expense me? I mean, even if they're not yours?"

"Sure." His voice softened. "I'll drive up there as soon as I can. Stay a couple days."

Carlotta grinned. Well, that would be a sweet deal. Jake was a good friend and sometimes more, but Damian was the one she cared most to be with. Damian stood up to the Haggerty harridans when they'd tried to shame her into moving out of town. If only she'd gotten that scholarship, a better education.

Damn Maude and Emily – spinsters from

nowhere now. Just dust in two graves, guarded by marble angels and splatters of bird poop. A better end than those two bitches deserved.

Carlotta waited in the waning light of dusk by the old church. Damian hadn't called, probably spending the day at work or with his wife and family. Had he contacted his research students about the bat mystery yet?

She shivered. This evening she wore a woolen muffler as well as her usual bat trekking attire. The chill still cut through her. God only knew how. At 38, old age couldn't be the problem. Well, Damian would warm her up. Perhaps he'd make the drive tomorrow, on Saturday. She hadn't seen him since the week before Halloween. He'd dressed as a vampire bat and made love to her, still in costume.

"Vampire bats never come to California," she had teased. "Some biologist you are."

He had nibbled on her nipples in reply. Then lower.

Ummm. Carlotta ached for the touch of Damian's hands and lips, the ecstasy from his exquisite thrusts. Compared with Damian, Jake screwed like he'd never learned how.

But the bats would awaken soon and escape the church to pursue insects. A few thousand bats coming to Pine Grove's vicinity on a whim creeped her out. Still, a promise to Damian was a promise. She'd go where there were fewer bats than in the church. She'd head for Jake's cabin before dawn to see if any of the critters showed up to roost in the crawl space under the roof. By sunrise she might get a closer look at the creatures' features. Or a closer look at Jake's if he had his way.

Faint sounds of movement in the dying daylight accompanied an even fainter high-pitched whine. Yes, a cloud of bats emerged from the church to feed. They glided and swooped with such grace, as though they didn't need to flap their wings at all. And they really were smaller than the usual bats that migrated here.

Five hundred? One thousand? Difficult to estimate the numbers. Dusk passed. The flying mammals disappeared into the night. Clouds closed in on the moon. Everything really turned dark, now. She switched on her halogen lantern. She should walk back to her driveway, move her 1990 Toyota Corolla to the graveyard and keep watch. Drive over to Jake's territory later on.

Carlotta carried her lamp by the handle and walked toward her car. Something brushed the back of her neck, pushed her wool scarf against her skin. What the hell? Her peripheral vision captured a glimpse of a low-flying creature, only a couple feet above the ground. A bat, a really small one sped away from her. Not a fruit bat, unless it had shrunk or mutated.

She reached her driveway, unlocked her Toyota and slid behind the steering wheel. Time to drive back to the graveyard as planned and bat watch from

the warmth of her car. The back of her neck felt odd. A tick? She touched the area. Damp and sticky. She slammed the car door and examined her hand in the lantern light. Blood coated her fingers. She removed her muffler. Blood stained the pale blue fabric, too.

The fucking animal had bitten her. How dared a bat bite her before she'd had her rabies booster? Shit. Shots always made her feel lousy. When Damian drove up here she wanted to feel her best, enjoy the full sensuality of his attention.

The cell phone in her pocket vibrated. A call from Damian.

"You owe me extra," Carlotta said. "One of your beloved bats bit me." She touched the back of her neck. "Jesus, I'm still bleeding."

"Bleeding?" His voice sounded odd.

"Yeah," she said. "I didn't even feel the thing bite."

"Have you been taking aspirin lately?" He cleared his throat. "Bruising easily?"

"No." She took a weekly low-dose aspirin, but that shouldn't matter.

"Listen," Damian said, "are you in your car?"

"Yeah," Carlotta said. She glanced at her darkened cottage and shoved her car key into the ignition. "I'm about to head to the old church."

"I'm going to drive up there tonight," Damian said, "as soon as I wrap up a few loose ends. Go back to your place. Right now. Forget about counting the bats. Forget about looking at the bats. Go home, then get inside as fast as you can. Keep the windows closed. Shut the insert in your fireplace, too."

"You trying to scare me?"

"Carlotta," he said, "Yes. I'm trying to scare you. So you won't do something stupid. I'm not sure there's anything wrong. Northern California isn't a normal or suitable habitat for vampire bats–"

"Vampire bats?" Carlotta asked. "What the hell–"

"Take a deep breath," Damian said. "Step out of panic mode. Vampire bats inject an anticoagulant – a sort of blood thinner – when they bite, but they aren't a threat to humans except for rabies. Whatever species of bat has turned up isn't behaving in a normal manner. Probably rabid and could carry other dangerous diseases. I don't want you to sustain any more bites."

"You'll be here by morning, then?" Her heart beat faster, yet not from the prospect of romance.

"I promise," he said.

"I love you," she whispered.

"I love you, too." Damian ended the call.

Her cell phone needed recharging. She closed the case and leaned back against the seat of her Toyota. Attack of the infected vampire bats. Great. All she needed. Damian wanted her to go home but didn't realize she parked in her own driveway. Carlotta already rolled up her windows. Maybe she should stay right here for the night.

Her stomach growled. She hadn't eaten much today. She reached into her backpack for a granola bar. Christ, she had to take a crap. Must be nerves. She touched the back of her neck which finally had stopped trickling blood.

Vampire bats lived in New Mexico's caves and farther south. Hadn't she read that somewhere? There

had to be a rational explanation why vamps had come to Pine Grove.

She really had to get to the bathroom.

The moon was out of the clouds now. No bats in sight. Regardless, Damian worried about diseases. She'd follow his advice and make a run for the front door of her cottage, thirty feet away.

Carlotta wound her wool muffler around her neck. Not much of her body was exposed. Only her face and hands, really. She pulled her house key out of her jean's pocket, pushed open the car door then lunged for the safety of her cottage.

Thirty feet to her house, twenty-five, twenty. Her boots thumped against the cracked, paved walkway. Only ten feet now. Something smacked into her cheek. A fucking bat.

She let out a scream, swatted the thing away and lunged forward. Her hand thrust her house key into the lock, pushed open the door, slammed the barrier shut behind her, then slid the chain lock. She gasped for air.

The escape was done, over, she was safe. Her fingers fumbled with the entryway light switch. Blood dripped from her face onto the throw rug. Jesus. Her stomach cramped. She hurried toward the bathroom.

Carlotta checked all her windows, the fireplace, any potential entrance to the cottage. She went from room to room, heart still pounding. Vampire bats weren't supposed to like light. Overhead lights, lamps, night lights, she turned them all on. Damian would arrive in a few hours. He was a bat guru. Everything would be all right.

The desk drawer. Damian's picture was in the desk drawer. Carlotta retrieved the photo and sat on the living room sofa. Damian was six-feet tall, square-shouldered and muscular, built like a lumberjack, really. His hair, curly in this old photo, had since thinned. She wanted him here now. Needed him more than his wife did. Carlotta was prettier than she, always had been. Someday Carlotta would have Damian for her own and paste their wedding photo on Emily Haggerty's tombstone.

Her cell phone vibrated. Not Damian's number this time. Jake Wilkin? He wasn't one to call and chat.

"Don't come up this way, tonight," Jake said, a twinge to his voice, like he'd been drinking more than usual.

"You okay?" Carlotta asked.

"Some whacked out bastard cut little holes," Jake said, "in my broodmare's hide. Anybody I catch near here tonight will eat ammo puddin.'"

"Be careful," Carlotta said. What would Jake do with a crazy story about vampire bats? "Some bats migrated in from out of state. They're not behaving normal. Probably rabid. I got bit an hour ago."

"Need me to come on down?" Jake asked.

"We both better stay put until sunrise," Carlotta said. Sweet of him to offer. "The professor of bats is on his way."

Carlotta slipped the cell phone back into her jeans

pocket. Something thumped against the living-room window. A heavier whump followed. The glass rattled. Carlotta's entire body tensed. Dear God. Something large – something dark – like an undulating blanket, charged the window. The thing hit the glass and retreated. No, two small objects – illuminated by the living room lamp – still pressed against the outside of the pane.

She clutched the unlit halogen lantern and moved toward the window. Two ugly, horrible, twisted faces, pulled together like puckered apples glared at her.

Holy mother, it couldn't be. Mustn't be. Carlotta staggered backward, away from the two bats, their facial features miniatures of Maude and Emily Haggerty's.

The black cloud swooped from night skies and assaulted the window. Battering rams of bats would smash the glass. Attack her. She had to go somewhere they couldn't reach. The bedroom closet. No, the closet had a flimsy ceiling panel leading to the attic crawl space. Carlotta might as well stand on the frigging front doorstep. But the bathroom had a sturdy door and a small window protected by curved wrought iron bars.

She grabbed her lantern and raced into the bathroom. Another thump. The living room window shattered. Carlotta slammed shut the bathroom door and turned the skeleton key, the one she always kept in the lock. A force hit the opposite side of the bathroom door. Lights went out.

Help. She had to call for help. Phone Damian, Jake, anyone she could. How could she tell the men that two bats looked like Maude and Emily Haggerty? That those bitches really had flown in from Hell?

She turned on her halogen lamp and fumbled for her cell phone. Shit, she needed to recharge. Nothing she could do about the batteries now. She called Damian and got his voice mail.

"They're in the house," she hollered into the telephone. "Help me, Damian. Do something."

She phoned 911. No answer there, either. Why didn't anyone answer? Next she left a message for Jake and prayed he'd pick it up soon. Not enough juice in the battery to make any more calls.

The pounding against the bathroom door intensified. Would the door collapse? How could little bats have so much strength, even with many working together?

But these bats weren't normal. Two of them had faces of the dead. Were they all supernatural? Attacking her at the bidding of the dead Haggerty harridans, an act of revenge for scandalizing their oh-so-dignified family name?

Weapons.

She needed weapons.

Hair spray. Tub and tile cleaner. A plumber's friend.

What good would those things do against killer bats? Maybe she could shield her face with towels.

Another sharp crack of glass breaking. The noise came from behind her.

Carlotta turned. Hundreds of tiny Maude and Emily faces leered with bared fangs through the jagged bathroom window. They had broken the

protected pane.

Haggerty bats squeezed between iron bars, flying at Carlotta's face – biting, tearing, swarming her head, her arms, ripping at her clothes, the creatures' high pitched whines like laughter. She screamed over and over, eyelids clamped shut, hands trying to shield her face and throat. She sank to her knees on the floor, rolled into a ball and kept screaming.

Screaming!

Gunfire outside. Voices shouted. No light, no people, just sounds. Had help finally come? Carlotta couldn't open her eyes. Her face felt like wet, sticky pulp. The room reeked of blood. Why couldn't she open her eyes? Did she even have eyes anymore?

"My God," Damian shouted. "My God."

Damian was here, somewhere beyond the broken window. Oh, blessed saints. Yet Carlotta couldn't answer, couldn't groan. Was she alive?

A man screamed. Damian? Then came guttural wails followed by an unearthly moan. Then nothing. Had the bats attacked him, too? Metal scraped metal. A doorknob rattled. Someone picked the lock. Footsteps traversed a creaking floor.

"Don't try to open yer eyes," a male voice said. Jake. "Don't try ta move at all." His voice lowered. "Help's a'comin', hon."

Pain, so much pain. Damian, she didn't hear him now. Was he all right? Someone squeezed her hand.

LAUREL ANNE HILL

Damian? Or Jake? The hand holding hers could be Damian's, couldn't it? He wouldn't let Maude or Emily get the best of him, keep him and Carlotta apart.

This had to be Damian. Had to be Damian. Had to be. . . .

LAUREL ANNE HILL has officially gone wicked. Although her award-winning novel, Heroes Arise (KOMENAR Publishing, 2007), stresses worthiness, a number of her recent short stories emphasize the darker side of human desires. "Worthiness has its rewards," Laurel says, "but unworthiness does, too. Rewards have many degrees and flavors." For nearly 20 years, Laurel has written science-fiction, fantasy, horror and short, narrative nonfiction. Her short works have appeared in a variety of publications. Several pieces have won awards. She is a member of California Writers Club, Broad Universe and Women Writing the West. Please visit her website and podcast at www.LaurelAnneHill.com.

greed

BY KIMBERLY STEELE
BEST IN BLOOD SEASON 3
HorrorAddicts.net Episode #28

"My name is Jim McGraw, and I'm an alcoholic."
Russell rolled his eyes, the sour aftertaste of a garlic pork chop gassing up his stomach. Did they have to state the obvious? The guy was fat, wheezy, and beads of sweat were visible on his sideburns, which was all that was left of the hair on his head. Dumb fuck.

The court ordered him to go to the meetings after he rear-ended a woman's car on a Wednesday afternoon. They threw the book at him because an eleven-month old on board was injured, knocked out a tooth or something. The paparazzi were all over it.

Within one week, the baby's face peered from tabloids everywhere, sporting a shiner and missing one tooth, along with Russell's stunned, corpulent mug shot and the rear-ended mom's ugly face. He wasn't even able to drive to his grandmother's funeral. He cabbed it.

Gram was finally dead. True to form, Mom wasn't upset, but with the amount of drugs (anti-depressant and otherwise) Mom gobbled morning and night, her arms and legs could be hacked off with a machete and she wouldn't feel much of anything.

Russell went a year without seeing Gram. The call arrived as a shock. Mom reported that Gram promised on her deathbed to gift Russell with her

most prized possession. Everyone knew Gram possessed an exquisite jewelry collection from her salad days. Gram was right up there with Lana Turner and Marlene Dietrich. Russell could sell any of that shit in a heartbeat. He almost salivated at the prospect. There was a blue sapphire necklace worth at least 700,000 dollars.

Even half a million would be fine. He was in a "spot of trouble" as his English friend, Mark, liked to put it. They auctioned off the contents of Russell's storage in New York because he forgot to pay. Suddenly pictures of his crap showed up in the Enquirer. Of course there was an early sex tape where he was blown by two sister heiresses at once. Now he stood to make zero money off of them and both of the fat-assed bitches' families were suing.

Russell was pissed. He had a bad feeling about the will reading, even though Gram always loved him and would provide for him in her will. He drove up to the lawyer's office, a severe, neat little place nestled in the recesses of a pretentious complex. His sister, Olivia, was there.

God, she had gotten fat. She looked like Mom and Gram, sort of, same coloring, except she was a butterball. Olivia's head was triangular and tiny atop pendulous breasts and an enormous convex stomach. There were no hips, just the torso tapering down to feet.

When Russell was fourteen and she was twelve, Olivia had a gorgeous body. Round breasts and a chiseled stomach appeared overnight. Russell started by snapping her bra and graduated to rubbing up against her boobs and groping her in the swimming pool when he got a chance. He had thought nothing of it and his parents looked the other way. Gram realized what was going on, took him aside, and threatened him. Gram told Russell he was never to touch his sister inappropriately again.

"But she's my sister," he had exclaimed.

"Exactly, Russell. She's your sister. She's off limits."

"I hate you!"

"If I find out you've touched her again, Russell, it won't matter that you're my blood."

Even at twelve, Russell knew not to mess with Gram. If disowned, Russell would no longer be the relative of a star. Young Russell imagined having no money, no connections, and no inheritance.

He was extra careful from then on. Gram distanced herself from Russell starting at age eight, right around the time he started playing video games.

Gram forbade Russell to play them in her house. Gram's huge mansion contained not a single TV. Instead, Gram had books. Walls and walls of them. Gram's bookshelves were so high that rolling ladders on tracks were the only way to get at them. Russell hated going to Gram's house because it was creepy and boring. His sister Olivia fucking loved it there. That's why she was Gram's favorite. Olivia loved to read. Her nose was always buried in a book. She had actually read War and Peace.

Russell tried to make it in the music industry. His band was booed off stage in Los Angeles and the tabloids ran with it. A couple of asshole news reporters said his album had an "unfinished, amateur"

quality, even though he spent nearly a million dollars for useless engineers to record and mix it. On top of that, tabloids claimed Russell had drug and alcohol problems just because of a few DUIs.

The lawyer ushered him into the cool office.

"Putting on some weight, aren't we, Russ?"

"Eat shit, Lemmond."

Gram had always ridden him about his weight. Never Olivia, even though she outweighed him by the time she was sixteen.

"Hi, Mom. Hi, Livvie." His mother walked up to him and hugged him weakly. Olivia stayed behind her, offering no physical contact. Olivia's big arms were crossed protectively over her ample breasts, her eyes puffy and swollen from crying.

Lemmond took two hours to read the will. Gram fancied herself something of a writer, even though other people penned her biographies. Russell suffered painfully through Gram's extended diatribe about valuing simple pleasures in life. Good friends, a beautiful sunset, a square meal in a world where so many were starving, blah, blah, blah. If Gram wasn't dead, Russell would have strangled her. Finally, they got to the money and possessions part.

"To my daughter, Kathleen, I leave nothing except advice. Stop taking enough pills to tranquilize a small elephant every day and night. You've already spoiled two children enough to ruin their lives. One can only hope that you'll either get clean or die by the time you have grandchildren, if you're so blessed."

Mom uttered a small "Ah," before staring off vacantly into space.

Lemmond kept reading. "To my grandson, Russell, I leave this advice. Stop thinking the world owes you a living, because it does not. Even though your mother and father could not seem to impart upon you the value of knowledge or the virtue of working to get a thing you want, it's never too late. To you, Russell, I leave my most prized possession, my deluxe hardbound folio of the Complete Works of William Shakespeare. Enjoy it, for it holds many secrets and riches.

Lemmond raised his eyebrows and cleared his throat. "To my beloved Olivia, I will always live in your heart. I leave to you the remainder of my estate, which includes the villa in Paris, the properties in New York, San Francisco, and Hilton Head, the library in Essex, the jewelry collection, the–

"This is bullshit," Russell exclaimed, pointing at Olivia. "She left everything to that fat fartknocker?"

Lemmond cleared his throat in response.

"I have the Shakespeare folio in my cabinet, would you like it now?"

"Fuck it. Just have her buried with it."

"She's to be cremated at the Nielsen Funeral Home on Thursday. Do you wish to have the book?"

"No." He stomped out.

Three days later, Russell's thumbs ached. Pizza boxes reached staggering heights upon the floor, nearly obscuring the profile of Russell's friend Mark sitting only three feet away. Cans of Coca-Cola grew mold deep inside aluminum terrariums as Russell prepared for a fiftieth round of Joe Madden Football. Russell recently snorted Ritalin to keep himself awake

for a week. The doorbell rang. Mark went to answer it.

"What do you want?" Mark asked.

"Just give this to my brother. It belongs to him."

Russell heard the door click shut. Mark brought him the Shakespeare folio. Heavy and thick, Mark held the folio in front of himself as if it were a baby. The folio's brown leather binding shined with polish. A red card, lovingly embossed with the title, Shakespeare's Plays, in gold, winked from the inlaid center of the book's cover. A gold lock and a purple pouch dangled from a rubber band.

"Looks like a key. Let's open it!"

"Open your butt crack. I'm not opening anything from that bitch."

"You're mad that your Gram didn't leave you anything?"

"What are you, stupid?"

"She left you a cool book!"

"She did it just to mess with me. The old cunt cut me out of her will except for this book, didn't you hear it in the tabloids yet? When she was dying, she called me an idiot. She said that I was a lazy, greedy slob who wouldn't crack a volume of Shakespeare if his fortune depended upon it."

"Oh, fuck. Let's open it!"

"No!"

"The key's right here!"

"We're going to the funeral home. Bring the book."

A wake going on in the funeral home made it easy for the two men to slip easily past the mourners down to the basement where bodies were prepared. Three other dead people besides Gram occupied the room. Mark went as white as a sheet upon seeing naked old people with blank plywood expressions.

"You know they have to put caps in their eyes, otherwise they sink in." Mark almost retched as he spoke.

Russell walked over to his grandmother. Her head was on a block. Tube-like breasts rested on either side of her ribcage. The embalmer hadn't even bothered sticking pasties on; what was the point when the boobs were trying to hide themselves under Gram's bony shoulders? He ripped off the handkerchief from his relative's crotch and giggled.

"Russell!" Mark looked around the room, paranoid. "What are you doing?"

"Hand me the book." Russell growled at his friend.

"Are you sure about this?"

"Hand me the book, fuckface."

Mark handed Russell the thick, heavy tome with no small measure of sadness.

Russell stuck the book between his grandmother's legs, wedging it in despite the rigor mortis.

"You shouldn't have done that." Mark sighed.

"Fire up the oven." Russell pointed to the corner of the room.

"The oven?"

"It's over there. What did you think it is? A fucking washing machine?"

"Why?"

"Gram's gonna get cremated early."

Much to Mark's dismay, Russell rolled his grandmother's gurney to the cremation oven.

"Help me. Grab her legs."

Mark, a steadfast conformist, obeyed orders.

Gram's bare shoulders were cold and clammy as Russell heaved her onto a rolling rack that helped convey bodies into the incinerator. Gram's head turned slightly as Russell manhandled her body, assuming an unnatural angle that seemed to accuse Russell from beyond death. Mark, visibly disturbed, remained silent.

Russell shoved Gram's head into the oven, the rolling rack clanking noisily.

"Push!" Gram's torso was fed to the oven. When she was slightly past the crotch, the book stopped her progress.

The stairs creaked and Mark jumped.

"Are you crying?" Russell asked.

"Sod off. I hope you get caught. I'm leaving." Mark let go of Gram's legs and flew up the stairs.

"Pussy." Russell heaved the book from his Gram's legs and stuffed the rest of her in the oven. Heat bellowed from the incinerator. The book was surprisingly flame-retardant, catching fire several minutes after Gram's body turned red and black.

Olivia stopped by the apartment again on

154

Saturday. The smell of Russell's ripe, yeasty garbage announced itself from the hallway. Olivia read a note from an irate neighbor pinned on Russell's door calling him a hoarder and threatening lawsuits.

Russell angrily abandoned unboxing his new PlayStation, bought shortly before his credit cards got cut off.

"What the hell do you want?"

"You can't even walk in here. It's disgusting."

"I didn't ask you to come in."

"Did you know that you're probably going to be arrested for what you did to Gram's body?"

"How did you know about that?"

"Mark told me."

"The fuck!"

"You're lucky that I'm not going to press charges, because I'll bet your prints are everywhere. They can get you on trespassing and destroying property even if I do nothing. You're in felony offense territory, you know."

"I can't believe he ratted on me!" Russell's face was livid with fury.

"You ruined Gram's wake. She was a star – did you ever think before you ruined her last goodbye to all of her fans?"

"I don't give a shit about her fans."

"Of course you don't. What did you do with the book?"

"I burned it with Gram."

"Wow, you are so dumb," his sister commented acidly, full cheeks blushing.

He readied himself to slam the door in her fat

face.

"Didn't you open the book, dumbass?"

"No. Fuck Shakespeare."

"You left the money in the book?"

"What money?" His heart nearly stopped beating for a moment.

"Like, I didn't count it all, but somewhere around, oh, I don't know, two point four million?"

""It was full of money?"

"She always said you wouldn't crack a volume of Shakespeare if your fortune depended on it! Oh, how stupid can a person be?"

"You opened my book!"

"Of course I opened it. I was planning on reading through Hamlet, I had hoped for some full color plates or old photos of Gram when she played Ophelia. Oh, this is just too funny."

He stood staring ice daggers at his sister, his head silently screaming over the two point four million dollars.

"It's your fault, Olivia! You need to give me a loan!"

"Maybe it was counterfeit, you know, Monopoly money. Gram liked a joke. I didn't look closely."

"Seriously, Livvie, can I hit you up for a hundred thousand? I'm kind of behind in my credit card payments right now, and you're a very rich woman."

"Go to hell. Don't call me, don't email me, and don't you dare come to my house or I will press charges, mark my word."

His sister stomped off as quickly as her large legs could carry her.

KIMBERLY STEELE

In the absence of his former gaming partner, Mark, Russell half-watched the setting sun while eating three-day old sausage pizza. He did not enjoy it.

KIMBERLY STEELE is the author of the first free vampire audiobook on the Internet, Forever Fifteen, which launched her out of obscurity in 2005. Today, Forever Fifteen has been downloaded nearly a million times. Kimberly's second vampire novel, River's Heart, is due for release in 2012. Kimberly lives with her husband and cat in Chicago, Illinois. Download the free Forever Fifteen audiobook at www.ForeverFifteen.com.

fallen

BY JENNIFER RAHN
Horror Addicts.net Episode #50

Tharn flared his gills and tasted the air carefully as he scanned the IR channel, not trusting the information supplied by Vo. Nothing showed up on the monochrome red of his scanner, not even rats or quagroaches, which usually meant poison or the presence of a bigger and meaner-than-average dumpsite squatter. Whatever had claimed this territory was probably nastier than he was, and therefore something he'd prefer not to confront. He clicked his scanner to another channel and still got nothing. "It's too quiet," he muttered.

Vo fidgeted and wiped his hands on his pant legs for the ninth time. "Whassa matter with you?" he snapped. "I told you, it's a good tip." His voice transducer buzzed annoyingly through his breathing mask. Humans didn't do so well with the levels of ammonia on this planetoid, and Tharn doubted the vintage unit Vo had strapped to his face was keeping all of it out.

"Then why didn't your tipster clear it out himself?"

"He's just a kid. I give him a cut for finding me these things. C'mon. It's a freebie, man."

"If he's already in, why bring me along?"

"Will you just shut up? Your share will be plenty and the kid is a net geek in a fuckin' wheelchair. I told you, it's good. Can we go already?"

Vo's sweating had gradually increased to the point where he looked leaky, which usually indicated he'd broken at least six of Tharn's Rules of Thievery. "You're not straight. You expect me to go in with you like that?"

"Ain't had none for a week!"

Meaning he was out of cash.

"I been sick, Tharn. Not everyone can regrow all perfect like you. I'm not all shiny blue-green-bald and scaly lizard-buggy perfect. Mister Supreme Being I'm-So-Indestructable, I'm an Underwater-Fish-God Guy. Mister Fuckin' Big-Huge-Blue-Bug-Eyes. Why the fuck don't you get a manicure? Oh, cuz you don't got the right number of fingers is why. Who only has two fuckin' huge nails like that?"

Humans. Frail and unreliable. "You're hurting. I can see you've got the shakes."

"We gonna do this?"

Tharn stared at the other thief for a long minute, trying to decide if there was something he was still lying about, or if he just looked that twitchy from drug withdrawal. Perhaps no roaches were here because this place really was that dead. So far off the map it was nothing but a huge waste of time. Vo probably hadn't been given a good tip, but they were here anyway. Maybe they could find enough scrap to buy lunch.

"All right." He let Vo take the lead, still not fully trusting that the area was clear. Something tickled at the edge of his senses. Something that didn't quite flare up his third eye, which he knew was working just fine, since it was telling him clearly that Vo hadn't eaten in two days, hadn't taken a crap in a week, and should probably stop in at a free clinic to get his ear infection treated and maybe get a shot of methadone.

They passed through heaps of detritus that looked like it used to be packing and hardware for a shipping line, and into what might have once been a warehouse. Didn't seem right that anything would still be here, since it already looked thoroughly picked over. They certainly weren't the first ones in. All he could hear was a constant drip of water, falling from the bent-in corrugated metal that used to be the ceiling, onto the concrete floor.

Vo stumbled ahead, confident in his information. Tharn followed behind with caution, senses on high alert.

"Y'could fuckin' help, g'damn, bug-faced, Caldoshan!"

He paused, ignoring Vo as the human tugged on a door that just wasn't moving. This was wrong. The way the air tasted inside, this place had been occupied, and less than a week ago.

Humans.

Armed.

Stealing whatever was hidden here would bring some major heat down on them, assuming they could even get past the electronic security he could now sense hiding in the walls.

"Vo–"

"Check it, Tharn! I told you!" Vo had gotten the door open and harsh light stung Tharn's eyes. His hearts froze and dropped into his stomach when he saw what lay behind. Several rows of shiny new guns

in brand new racks sat in their controlled and well-lit environment.

"Vo, you dumb shit."

A gun barrel stabbed against the back of Tharn's head and at the same time a round clicked into its chamber. "Tha's righ', Sunshine. He's as dumb as you look. Now, face down. Nice and slow."

Tharn didn't try to hold on as he felt his scanning gear get ripped out of his hands and someone pushed him down onto the concrete.

Vo was also being hogtied by soldiers – Quadstar Marines by the look of their armor. "This place was supposed to be clean," he squealed. He still didn't get it.

"It's military, dumbass! No one's gonna leave this much high-end shit out here unguarded!"

"Why didn't you say, Tharn! Why didn't you smell them?"

Tharn lost interest in the conversation as the marines shoved his head down and snapped a suppressor grid onto the back of his neck. He felt nanowires snake through his blue scales and into his brain stem, shutting down his third eye. He screamed as his mind went blind, and he tried to scrape his visual eyes against the concrete to make them work better.

"You're fine, Sunshine." Someone shoved a rag in his mouth. "Quit bellyachin'."

Fine? Fine? These blind-ass humans had no idea what suppressor grids were like. He struggled against his wrist-clasps, whipping his head back and forth, as he was bumped and dragged along, trying to get the damned thing off. Nothing could be trusted now, what he heard or smelled or saw – it was all suspect because he couldn't know.

The cargo hatch of a military freighter opened with a sucking hiss, and he and Vo were dumped onto the metal grid flooring, hands and mind still bound. The entire structure beneath him shook violently, gradually smoothing out as they reached orbit. Over the relentless roar of engines, Vo was saying something to him. Something like, "Hey. Hey . . . Tharn? You gonna be all right? Tharn?"

He couldn't answer, and just kept rubbing the back of his head against the metal floor, trying to rub the grid off.

"You're starting to bleed, man. I know you grow back and stuff, but c'mon. Cut it out. Hey! Hey! You guys got a medic? I need a medic in here!"

All sound bleached from Tharn's experience as his entire body tried to reject the nanowires binding his senses. Maybe Vo had stood up. Maybe he had started rattling his chains. For sure he got shot in the head, because Tharn was usually not wrong when he tasted blood and brains in the air. Shock and self-preservation made him start listening again.

"What about the other one?" The light-voiced speaker kicked him in the back.

"Who gives a fuck?" A deeper voice. A drawl from the Outer Mining Belt. "It's a Civie matter. I don't care about that shit."

"Then why'd we pick 'em up in the first place?"

"Had to run 'em through the scanner. They're not coded, so who cares? No one's gonna notice when

they're gone."

"Want me to shoot him too?" Sounded like some kid. Was that guy older than twelve? Why was he even allowed in the Marines?

"Toss him out the airlock. Less messy. And clean up that other shit."

Thanks, Outer Mining Belt Guy! Like to see you try it when my hands aren't bound!

"Hey, private, go get a mop." A woman this time.

"Why me?"

"Naw, it's yes, sir, not why you. Go get a fuckin' mop."

Geez, she must have a complex about something.

Tharn snarled and wrenched against his bonds, but he really was getting tossed out of an airlock. The soldiers cleared out and he felt the vibrations of an inner door clanging shut. The floor he lay on tilted downward, opening to an intense cold toward which all the air was rushing, dragging him into blackness. Vo's faceless body tumbled past, twisting like flypaper and rupturing inside out when it hit the vacuum.

Tharn felt like it was happening in slow motion, giving him time to cover his eyes with nictitating membranes, shift his scales to harden his flesh, close his gills and nose flaps, and finally, slow down his hearts. He curled into a ball as his own body was sucked into the sudden, soul-chilling silence. Still, he was all right. He was a seed. This was how his ancestors had emigrated from the Oceans of Caldosh in the first place, maybe losing limbs or flesh, but his kind could partially regenerate such things. Maybe the extreme cold would break the grid still clamped on his neck, and when he finally landed somewhere and awoke, he'd be set to rights again.

Gravitational pull.

Wasn't this . . . soon?

Yup.

Happening fast. Entering orbit. Gonna hit the air.

The sudden temperature shift on Tharn's scales forced him to wake up, and his mind reeled with the momentum of hurtling through the thin atmosphere towards the surface of whatever had caught his insignificant mass. He tried to open his third eye to see where he was headed, and it took him a few seconds to remember that the suppression grid remained clamped to his brain stem. He twisted his arms against the cold-damaged wrist-clasps and finally managed to wrench them open so he could claw at the back of his neck. The grid housing came away in his fingers. The nanowires did not.

Fuck.

With nothing to anchor them, the damned things were twisting through his body. He hoped they wouldn't get to his hearts. But his third eye opened, just an inch.

Two seconds before impact, he realized where he was –the Tranx Penal Asteroid. The blue metal walls of the main prison structure, and the stylized skulls engraved in them, had been the stuff of cheap comic holos and B-rated vamp movies that every kid knew. Spikes and barbed wire decorated the balustrades, now rusting to scrap in the corrosive atmosphere.

Rumors had swirled about convicts deemed incapable of reintegration into society being left

behind during the decommissioning of this prison 15 years ago. The humans had been up in arms, as if they actually cared about their own species. The prison administration denied everything, claiming all inhabitants had been relocated, but then, Vo's warehouse was also supposed to have been empty.

So here he was, hurtling towards more uncertainty and an impact that would be his body mass multiplied by gravitational acceleration. . . .

Damned humans and their stupid frying pans and fires.

He flailed in free fall, trying to glide in, but just managed to slant his trajectory enough to end up skidding for half a kilometer – instead of smashing his skull on the none-too-soft ground – earning himself a face full of dirt.

Nanowires snaked around under his scales, forming raised patterns stained purple by his blood, and it fucking hurt. He got up and staggered towards the wrecked gates of the prison, spitting out blood and earth, trying to force his third eye open even more.

The atmosphere had ammonia and sulfur in it, making it distasteful, but not impossible for a Caldoshan to breathe. He filtered the air through his gills rather than draw it into his lungs, where it would scorch him as badly as it would any human. The Tranx mythos had contained many a tale of human escapees trying to flee without breathing masks, only to burn to death from their insides.

With that grim thought, he punched himself through the air lock and sighed in relief that the air recyclers were still operational. He flexed his gills to clear out the stench, then took a deep breath with his lungs, enjoying the oxygen rush. He hoped there were at least remnants of a medi-station here. Maybe some painkillers if he were lucky.

A humanoid ran past an unlit hallway off to the left.

Aw, shit. Of course there would have to be some nut-job still here. Well, it meant there was food.

Heaving a sigh, still frustrated that his third eye was not fully opening, Tharn went to hunt the human down. Survival here would have been difficult, so there was a high probability he'd find himself dealing with some psycho murderer who had out-competed all other criminal life left behind.

The inner halls had the recyclers running full blast, and the heat was up. The place still stunk – he wasn't sure of what. Security monitors were fully powered and scanning the entire compound – or they were until the lights went off.

Tharn snorted derisively. He flared his gills to just smell the human out. He didn't need to see by light.

A monitor at the back of the room flickered on, showing just static, then a dim black-and-white image of his new roommate, who seemed to think it was attractive to show off his tonsils and broken teeth as close to the camera lens as possible. Or maybe he thought it was funny, considering how hard he was laughing. His voice sounded tinny through the warped speakers, grating on Tharn's already raw nerves.

"Look! Look!" He gasped. "I was saving this.

Saving it for something special." He wasn't the only one there. He pulled up the head of a smaller human by the hair, shoving the guy's face into the camera. "Oh, God. Oh, God. I'm so happy. This one's broken." He stopped for a few seconds to catch his breath. "I don't need it anymore now."

The psycho romped around his room a couple times, then came back to the camera with a curved shard of honed metal. "See? You can watch. But only because I like you." He grabbed the other human's hair and forced him close to the camera again. The guy had a slight smile on his face, but otherwise looked resigned as Psycho slit his throat and rubbed his own face in the blood, turning at intervals to scream and laugh into the camera.

Tharn sighed. Like he needed this.

"Right behind you!" Psycho screamed and came rushing towards Tharn, smacking him across the face with a pipe, just as he turned.

Crazy human had just been one room over. Tharn grabbed Psycho's arm and twisted, intending to break it when the human tossed a fistful of neurodust in his face – the kind that was meant to subdue Caldoshans.

Wasn't this just a human prison? Where'd he get that stuff? Doubt led to a trickle of fear – this scale-less pink bastard might actually be a threat. The dust burned slightly as he brushed at his face, trying to get it off, ignoring the annoying, wheezing laugh coming from the human skipping just out of reach. His skin and throat grew numb, and black spots formed in his vision.

Tharn went down with Psycho's weight on top of

him. His limbs stiffened and his body seized, making it impossible for him to retaliate. His head spun and the overwhelming stench of blood and halitosis made him gag.

Psycho was dragging him somewhere, strapping him down on a table, constantly giggling and repeating "Oh, God," until Tharn thought the guy was going to piss himself. As soon as his body metabolized this stupid dust, he was going to–

His head was locked into a clamp and tilted back, giving him the distinct impression he was not going to like what came next.

Psycho moved into his blurred view. "I'm going home," he said, his voice sounding like a reverberating echo. "Going home. Mamma's been waiting."

The sound of a laser drill made Tharn panic enough to fight his way through the drug-induced haze, part of his mind still not believing what was happening. He saw the light touching the scales of his chest, sparks fluttering around the beam, then the acrid stench of vaporized keratin hit. He watched in horror until the beam cut through and he flinched as it scorched his flesh underneath, making him thrash uselessly against the restraints.

Psycho kept the beam moving upward until he had cut open his throat. Peeling the skin and scales aside, he cut open Tharn's larynx and began scraping around the inside with a rusty scalpel. Tharn gagged reflexively and choked as his breathing organ was detached from the outer skin of his gill openings.

A Caldoshan could not regrow seven particular body parts, and that was one of them. Was this really

happening? Without it he'd only be able to use his lungs, and be unable to breathe outside the prison. Escape would be as impossible for him as it had been for the humans left here to rot.

Tharn tried to scream, but it was too late. He was mute, and all he could do was suck air in through the gaping hole in his neck, choking on blood being drawn in from his wounds.

He passed out for brief intervals, waking to see Psycho using nanotech to wire the breathing organ to his own throat, cutting away pieces of himself to make room, making mocking grimaces of pain and dropping his own flesh with taunts onto Tharn's face.

Psycho slapped him awake again to hold up a Caldoshan unborn and explain something about using stem cells to generate neural attachments to his fake gills, then stuffed the unborn into his mouth, and chewed. That wouldn't work, would it? Psycho injected himself with an oversized syringe of something green, constantly muttering, "Mutagen. Mutagen."

When Tharn woke again, the restraints had been removed, and he was lying in a cold patch of sticky blood. The pain in his throat made it too difficult to lift his head, so he rolled to his side and carefully pushed himself upright, feeling as if he should gag, but missing the muscles to do so. His hands went to the empty place at his neck, but he could not bring himself to touch it. He reached for a semi-clean towel and held it over the hole so that he would not see it, should he pass by a reflective surface.

A monitor flickered on as he passed by. Psycho's

face appeared.

"Caldoshan? I'll be gone by the time you hear this. I'll have gone home." More irritating giggling. "Like my new set up?" He gestured at the organic and nanotech abomination he was wearing around his neck. "Works great. Now I can get to the escape pods those nasty jailers left here, but juuuuuust out of reach! Too far away to run to while holding my breath. I know. I tried. Home. I didn't kill you, because . . . I'm too nice. Have fun breathing the atmosphere outside the prison. I know I did." He giggled. The screen shut off.

Tharn took a few moments to identify the emotion that filled him to the point where his skin felt tight and his hearts felt overrun – murderous rage. He was not going to be trapped here while that Psycho escaped with his breathing organ! He slowly stumbled around the medi-station, at last seeing what was scattered around it, and realizing humans had been hiding some sort of anti-Caldoshan bioweapons lab here.

Several vials of Caldosh-specific viral mutagens sat in a glass case – the same stuff Psycho had injected himself with. Perhaps it was unreported experimentation, since the authorities hadn't known to come clean up the evidence. At least it explained where Psycho had gotten the drugs and unborn.

Tharn stood with one of the thawed embryos in his hand, staring at its small, unformed features.

No fucking way!

This was not over. He was going to find a way to breathe through the toxic barrier outside, find

Psycho, and . . . and. . . .

The rage building within his thoughts made him dizzy and he gripped the counter to keep from falling.

Stem cells in the unborn. Could he do it? Tharn held one of the small forms in front of his opened mouth . . . and promptly vomited then passed out.

He woke up shortly, struggling to breathe. He clawed away the vile gunk coating his nose, mouth and hole in his neck – which all burned painfully, and nearly passed out at the sensation of cold, fresher air rushing into his lungs, along with the metallic tang of fresh blood.

He did his best to control his despair and nausea as he fumbled his way towards a large metal sink and used the rusty water to clean up. His sanity slid a bit as he had to force himself to stare at the unnatural opening in his throat and flush it out enough to stop the burning retches, choking on the water as he did so. Reality crept back in. What did he really think he could do? A filter mask would have been all he needed, but if there had been one here, Psycho would have used it eons ago. He was going to die here, and that was the end of it.

In his frustration, Tharn smashed the mirror with his fists, then couldn't stop. The computer consoles, the medicine cabinets, the surgical tables – anything that came into contact with his hands he tore apart.

His hands were bleeding. Shards of metal and glass fell from his fingers and arms, his blood turning from purple to blue as it fell to the floor.

Blue? That didn't seem good.

His nose and throat were swelling. A half-torn

biohazard label on what had been an intact mutagen container caught his eye.

Oh, shit!

Some of the scattered unborn didn't seem so dead anymore. Tharn blinked in disbelief unable to move as an embryo lifted its proportionately too-large head and turned a gooey white cornea in his direction. His sense of self-preservation battled with the need of his sanity to prove to him that what he was seeing was not real. He had to be hallucinating. If he stared at it for just a moment longer, he would properly interpret what he was actually seeing.

The little slime-covered chicken in front of him opened its beaky mouth and shrieked before jumping at his face and jabbing its stem-cell ridden tentacles into his head. His face felt like it was being ripped apart and stretched in several unintended directions.

The drugs are making me – no, it's the pain. Oh, God! Wake up, Tharn. This is not happening. Dead things don't move. Not like this.

Through the gaps between the embryo's tentacles that didn't quite cover his eyes, he could see others get up and move. Several more jumped onto his face, jabbing tentacles into his ears, nose, and cheeks. He couldn't breathe. They had closed over the hole in his neck and he fell to the ground but didn't feel any sort of impact.

He felt like he had bounced off a rubber spring board coated with moss . . . blue-green algae from a swamp on Caldosh, rushing over him with the waves of water he plummeted into . . . that's where he was. Perhaps.

Psycho was there, laughing and squealing, not letting him rest. Wait. Only he was here. But that couldn't be his voice, because his larynx had been removed, and his breathing organ lost. The embryos were crawling all over his body, changing him. Making him grow. . . .

Caldoshans. We regenerate. We want to go away. Not left here. Never supposed to have come here in the first place. Lying humans stole us, changed us. Made Us. Trapped.

Who are–

We are . . . together now.

Tharn's mind left him. Maybe he died.

Breathing again. Good, yes. Seeing again, third eye open, very good. Opening door, see outside. Go outside. It's okay. Dark, swirly poison. Outside and still alive. Can breathe! Can't. Can't hurt anything now. Got new, uh, yes, new gills. Not the same as before, but it doesn't matter. Allllll these little mutated embryos making it so easy! Can't stop a regenerated Caldoshan. Stupid Psycho. Oh, God! Making it to the launch pads. Made it. Who is that? Reflected in the glass? Damn, he looks fucked up. Did he eat embryos too? Must have, must have done something, because that's not natural what he's got going on there. Not natural. Get inside. Control center. Maybe, maybe, maybe. Yes! Transport logs recorded everything. Psycho should have, um. He should have destroyed the other four after launch, but didn't. Now Tharn gets one too. Who is Tharn? Doesn't matter. Leaving now.

Cold. Dark. Long ride. Long ride, um, home.

That's Mamma? Shouldn't that be her? Oh, Psycho's Mamma. Not pleased to see Tharn. All good, because this was home and – oh, God – it was her place to be mother and she'd do it, she'd do it, whether she wanted to or not. Because . . . because . . . well, who the fuck cared what because. She'd just do it because.

Oh, God!

Psycho! How did he get here, how did he? Oh, God! Followed him, remember? That's why. Read the transport logs and followed him. Must have. Hee hee!

There were five pods. He should have, should have, um, should have destroyed the other four after launch, but didn't. Didn't and now bug-eyed Caldoshan guy has come.

Where is Psycho going? He needs to be more polite to his guests.

Mamma is screaming. Make her be quiet. Bite her. Bite her face, make her quiet. Oh, God. Yuck. Don't want to eat. Embryos still moving. Really? Look at that. Coming off and moving to Mamma. Look at her grow. Oh. Hello, Psycho. Back again?

"Did he eat you, Mamma?"

He sounds scared. How strange. Look at him, gone and gotten Papa's gun hidden in the attic. He thinks he's gonna git that alien. Huuuhhhhh. Kill him first, proper now. Go get Go. Go get 'im.

"Did you. . . ? Blast you all to hell, fucker!"

Ohh, he's mad now.

Blam!

Blam!

Blam!

Out of bullets now, but, but, oh, God! Hee hee heeeeeeeeeeee! Can't be dead. Tharn's from Caldosh. Can't be dead from a little thing like that. But can't move right now, lying on the floor. Just give it a minute. Stupid, Psycho. Should have picked his victims better.

"Mamma? You're changing. He's spat green mutagen all over you. Now you've got big teeth like alien guy. Mamma? What are you. . . ? Why are you looking at me like. . . ?"

Look at him, shifting like he's not so sure anymore. He's gonna scream in just a second. Wait for it. Wait.

"Oh, God!"

Good bye, Psycho. Was not nice knowing you.

Hey, Mamma, save a little bit for me.

JENNIFER RAHN is the author of the dark fantasy novels, The Longevity Thesis and Wicked Initiations. She also has short stories in Dragon Moon Press' "Podthology," and Space Puppet Press's "Strange Worlds" anthology. Jennifer has degrees in Pharmacology and Medical Sciences, and currently works in academia and the biotech industry. Find out more about Jennifer at: www.LongevityThesis.ca.

cover art

BY MASLOSKI CARMEN

Masloski Carmen's passion for art has traveled through her veins since childhood. The love for art has increased with age, and the progress of her work, turning a hobby into expression through "digital art." Her creations are becoming increasingly popular, and Masloski is collaborating with other artists, writers, bloggers and many others, and her artwork is being featured in some European Digital Art Galleries.

To view more of her work, please visit:
http://goh665.daportfolio.com
or
http://mskycarment.deviantart.com

acknowledgements

*H*orrorAddicts.net and I would like to thank all the listeners and readers that support us, comment on our blog, participate on our Facebook page, and help spread the news that we exist. We'd like to thank Michele Roger for starting the Wicked Women Writers group, without which these stories might have never been told. To all the Wicked Women Writers and the editor, Hollie Snider, thank you for supporting the charity LitWorld. org. To Masloski Carmen, thank you for the use of your beautiful cover art. We fell in love with it the first moment we saw it. Your work is breathtaking. To all those new to the HorrorAddicts.net world, welcome! We have much more to offer you and hope you will become part of the fold.

~Emerian Rich, HorrorAddicts.net Hostess

I would like to thank Michele Roger for creating the Wicked Women Writers and giving us a virtual place to gather. I would like to thank the listeners who spread the word about our annual contest and support our efforts to entertain horror fans around the world. I would also like to thank Emerian Rich for hand-selecting the stories in this anthology and making my job easier. I hate sending out rejection letters! Thanks to Masloski Carmen for letting us use her artwork for our beautiful cover. And, finally, thanks to the readers and listeners, new and old, for supporting Horror Addicts, the Wicked Women Writers and LitWorld.org. Welcome to our playground!

~Hollie Snider, Editor

Check out these other titles from our

Wicked Women Writers

NIGHT'S KNIGHT'S by Emerian Rich
Vampires on a quest for knowledge attempt to create the perfect offspring, but from the shadows an even more demonic evil threatens their immortality.

THE MARK OF A DRUID by Rhonda R. Carpenter
An ancient Celtic prophecy and long sought-after revenge entangles the past with the present in the struggle for existence that threatens to destroy her project. A druidess and a shape-shifter must join together to save the Druid way of life, while a Queen conspires to kill Erin's only High King.

HEROES ARISE by Laurel Anne Hill
In a world where justice is achieved through careful customs of vengeance, a noble being pursues love and the preservation of his honor.

THE FOX by Arlene Radasky
A fascinatingly sublime historical romance and fantasy novel that looks at true courage and truly selfless acts. In this epic fiction that crosses centuries, Druid healers at the beginning of recorded time will be rescued from obscurity by an archeologist of the twenty-first century.

WICKED INITIATIONS by Jennifer Rahn
King Vladdir is cursed with cannibalistic desires by the capricious, dark magic of the Desert. However, his true enemy is the mysterious Desert Priest, who taps into Vladdir's curse to ensure the King will never know peace, and will lose all he holds dear.

LIVE AND LET UNDEAD Edited by Hollie Snider
The Zombie-pocolypse is real! Loved ones are returning from the grave in search of flesh and brains! Humans are running scared! Aren't they? Well, not so much. Here, rather than shooting them in the head, eighteen talented authors have figured out how to put the Undead to work. zombies can now be contributing members of society once more. Some funny, some horrific and some heart-breaking, these stories, from 18 talented authors, will leave you wishing for a zombie of your own. Maybe. . . .

DREAM OF THE ARCHER by Linda Ciletti

Lenore wants only to fulfill her grandfather's dying wish and visit his homeland, England. But her dream quickly turns into a nightmare as the magic of centuries past crosses time and thrusts her into medieval Sherwood Forest – a time where beautiful women are acquisitions and good people are punished for being poor. Damian d'Armante returns from war in the Holy Land only to find that his family lands have been confiscated by the Sheriff of Nottingham. Damian joins Robyn Hode's band of vigilantes. He wants his lands back. But first he needs to rid himself of the dark dreams that plague him nightly. Dreams of a fair-haired angel leading him to his death. Or is it a dream?

THE CONSERVATORY by Michele Roger

Hillford Conservatory is known for turning out star after star in the world of music. But what the new teacher, Melody, discovers in the school's secret, experimental genetic lab is that Dean Harwell uses more than theory and practice to create his icons. And when the experiments go terribly wrong, it is the students who suffer from the monstrous mistakes.

DREAMING OF DELIVERANCE by R. E. Chambliss

Lindsay Paulson is halfway through a 10-year prison sentence when she begins having what seem to be dreams that she leaves her cell in the night and visits another reality called Trae. Dreaming of Deliverance tells of Lindsay's experiences in Trae, where people are enslaved by terrifying creatures, and in prison, where she has to deal with fear, loss, and betrayal. During Lindsay's visits to Trae she discovers an inner-strength, a powerful, bitter-sweet love, and finally hope for both Trae's people and herself.

FOREVER FIFTEEN by Kimberly Steele

Lucy Albert is not your ordinary maladjusted suburban adolescent. Born into the era of the Black Plague in medieval Italy, Lucy is chosen as a mate by the sinister vampire Sebastianus against her will. Struggling to survive in a modern world she cannot identify with, Lucy isn't looking for attention. Welcome to Forever Fifteen, where a lonely girl seeks refuge in a world awash in everyday brutality, a world where only blood and death can sate her hunger.

Find these titles and more at the HorrorAddicts.net shop.

HORRORADDICTS.NET

HORRORADDICTS.NET

Do you love horror?
Want to hear a podcast created by
horror fanatics just like you?
Listen to HorrorAddicts.net.

Real horror reported by real horror fans.
We cover the news and reviews of horror:

☠movies	☠games	☠books
☠manga	☠anime	☠music
☠comics	☠locations	☠events
☠rpgs	☠fashion	☠more!

Every episode features horror authors, podcasters, movie people, musicians, and horror personalities.

Featuring the annual Wicked Women Writers and Masters of Macabre Challenges, the reality sitcom GothHaus, 100 Word Stories, and music from www.graveconcernsezine.com

Your one stop horror source:

HORRORADDICTS.NET

Maslocki Carmon

Rhonda Carpenter

Michele Popper

Mark Breen

Hollie Snieder

Laurel Anne Hill

Jennifer Rahn

R. E. Chambliss

Radusky

Kimberly Hunter

Linda Cilette

Jeri Unselt

Erin Rich

Sophie

Heather Roulo

LitWorld

LitWorld's mission is to use the power of story to cultivate literacy skills in the world's most vulnerable children.

LitWorld advocates for literacy as an urgent human right that belongs to every child.

LitWorld is a 501C3 non-profit organization led by renowned literacy advocate and author Pam Allyn. The LitWorld team is composed of literacy activists, educators, poets, storytellers, writers, and change-makers whose breadth of talent and inspiration has led to the creation of innovative literacy curricula and resources. LitWorld partners with children, parents, community members, teachers, and organizations that share LitWorld's values to support the development of sustainable literacy practices across the world.

Visit litworld.org to join the Global Literacy Movement.